The Return of Raffles

I stood silently while he bent an ear to the safe, his fingers dexterously twisting the dial, as he played with the combination. It seemed only a moment before there came a tell-tale click and, with a sigh, Raffles swung the safe door open. From the pocket of his overcoat he produced a small black cloth sack.

'Hold on to this a moment, Bunny,' he ordered, and, as I did so, he shone his torch into the interior of the safe. 'Great stuff!' he chortled, his arm reaching in and coming out with a tiny golden object in his fingers.

'Stand still! The game is up!'

The raucous voice echoing in the room froze me to the spot. Suddenly the lights blazed on and the french windows and the door seemed to spew forth policemen.

Raffles swung round open-mouthed. Even in my petrified state I observed that he had an expression of utter astonishment on his usually well-controlled features.

A heavy, red-faced man in an ulster and bowler hat came up and stood, hands on hips grinning in triumph at us.

'Well, well, well. *Mister* Raffles and *Mister* Manders. At long, long last. I've finally got the goods on you!'

There was no mistaking the Scottish burr in his voice. I nearly passed out in my agitation as I met the malignant gaze of our old arch-enemy – Inspector Mackenzie of Scotland Yard . . .

Also by Peter Tremayne

THE FIRES OF LAN-KERN
DRACULA, MY LOVE
THE REVENGE OF DRACULA

PETER TREMAYNE

The Return of Raffles

SEVERN SH HOUSE

This first hardcover edition published in Great Britain 1990 by
SEVERN HOUSE PUBLISHERS LTD of
35 Manor Road, Wallington, Surrey SM6 0BW.
First published in paperback format only 1981 by
Magnum Books

This title first published in the U.S.A. 1991 by
SEVERN HOUSE PUBLISHERS INC of
271 Madison Avenue, New York, NY 10016

British Library Cataloguing in Publication Data
Tremayne, Peter *1943–*
  The return of Raffles
  Rn: Peter Beresford Ellis I. Title
  823.914 [F]

  ISBN 0–7278–4140–8

Distributed in the U.S.A. by
Mercedes Distribution Center Inc.
62 Imlay Street, Brooklyn, NY 11231

Printed and bound in Great Britain
by Bookcraft (Bath) Ltd.

BIBLIOGRAPHICAL NOTE

Sir Arthur Conan Doyle told his brother-in-law Ernest William Hornung (1866–1921) that if he made the hero of his books a thief they would not be successful. Hornung ignored the advice and went ahead with the creation of Arthur J. Raffles 'a gentleman burglar'. Eight stories appeared as *The Amateur Cracksman* in 1899 and a further eight stories appeared as *The Black Mask* in 1901. Subsequently these stories were published in one volume as *Raffles, The Amateur Cracksman* in 1906. Further stories appeared in *A Thief in the Night*, 1905, and a full-length Raffles' adventure appeared as *Mr Justice Raffles* in 1909. Chronologically, however, the sequence is *Raffles, Mr Justice Raffles* and *A Thief in the Night*.

Raffles, like Sherlock Holmes, achieved a special place in literary criminology.

At the end of *A Thief in the Night*, Bunny Manders, Raffles friend and fumbling, unwilling accomplice, returns to London after being wounded in the Boer War in 1900. Raffles is believed to have been killed in the war. Bunny renews his friendship with a young lady who knew his secret and forgave him and, a reformed character, he settles down to a new life.

But was that the end of Raffles and their adventures together . . .?

CHAPTER ONE

The iron poker felt hot and clammy in my hand.

For a moment I paused irresolute halfway down the carpeted staircase which led into the threatening twilight of the great hall. My heart was pounding like the pistons in a steam engine and I was sweating in spite of the fact that I was standing in my bare feet and clad only in cotton pyjamas, not to mention the fact that two o'clock in the morning is not the warmest of hours to go abroad scantily clad.

A voice was still echoing in my head. Henry Manders, old fellow, it was saying coaxingly, stop this nonsense at once! Why don't you forget that you've been woken up by some mysterious noise? Why don't you just turn around and go back to your nice warm bed? Just lock your door, old man, and pretend that you haven't heard a thing.

I was very receptive to such advice but, at the same time, a second voice was interrupting this flow of thought. In my youth I was cursed by a pious uncle, an Anglican clergyman no less, who was fond of admonishing me on the follies of youthful sin. I'll swear that it was his voice, stern and rebuking so far as any nasal treble can be, telling me it was my duty to continue down the stairs to the study from whence the noise had issued.

Henry! Henry Manders! came that awful tone. You are a guest in your brother-in-law's house. There is no one else in the house. He is out and all the servants have been given the night off except old Thomas, and he is as deaf as a garden post. Someone is in the study! A burglar! Someone is trying to break into your brother-in-law's safe! Will you stand idly by and let your brother-in-law be robbed?

It would be wrong of me to deny the fact that I am not by

any means a bold person. However, the urgings of my conscience, albeit in the guise of my clergyman uncle, thankfully long departed, one hopes, to a better place, caused me to press forward down the stairs.

I would have said that the burglar, if such there was, must surely have heard me coming, so loudly did my heart pound against my ribs.

I reached the bottom of the stairs and started across the hallway towards the study-door. Even in the gloom of the hall I saw that it was slightly opened and saw the quick stab of a torch beam in the room behind.

So there was a burglar!

Raising my poker in a trembling hand, and holding my breath, I pushed the study door gently forward.

A figure was crouched against the far wall where I knew my brother-in-law kept his safe. It was shrouded in a heavy overcoat, and its back was towards me as one hand played with the combination dial on the safe while the other directed the torch beam to illuminate the work.

Now I had suddenly gone cold. For a moment I felt like stone, unable to move. I bit my lip hard to cause some reaction and forced myself quietly into the room.

Thank God my brother-in-law's house was fitted with the new electric light. It was with such a prayer that I reached out to the wall and let my hand move over the switch.

Then, with a cry of 'Hands up!', which probably scared me as much as it did the figure crouched by the safe, I flicked on the lights.

The man by the safe whirled round.

A white face met mine. A handsome face with a broad forehead, a humorous mouth and brown eyes that now stared in a startled fashion at me. I had last seen that face nearly four years ago: four years ago on the sunbaked veld before Mafeking in South Africa. Its owner was lying splashed in blood and a sergeant was dragging me away, telling me that 'the awficer be dead, sor' and that we'd best save ourselves while we had the chance.

In my shock I dropped the poker, staggered a couple of steps towards the nearby chaise-longue.

'Raffles!' I gasped before I tumbled down a well of velvet blackness.

CHAPTER TWO

'Come on, Bunny, old fellow,' said a well-known voice from a distance of what seemed several miles away. 'Drink this up, like a good chap.'

There was a smell of brandy under my nose and something cold and hard was pressed against my lips. A fiery liquid seeped into my mouth and throat.

I coughed and suddenly sat up rigid.

Standing gazing down at me, an amused expression on his saturnine face, was A. J. Raffles. Raffles, England's greatest cricketer and, if the truth were known, her greatest amateur cracksman. But Raffles had been killed in the Boer War in 1900, four years ago!

He must have anticipated my thoughts.

'No, old chap,' he said quietly. 'I'm not a ghost. As you can see, Bunny old thing, A. J. Raffles is still very much in the land of the living.'

I could do nothing but gurgle inarticulately for a while.

Raffles in the meantime, as nonchalantly as if I had seen him the day before and merely joined him for an after dinner drink at his club, was pouring himself a brandy from the silver encased cut-glass decanter on the sideboard and gazing ruefully at the safe which he had been trying to open.

'I knew I had left it too long,' he said, a tone of regret in his voice. 'I must be losing my touch.'

He looked down at his finger tips with mock distaste.

I simply sat and stared as he then drew forth a long silver cigarette case, took from it a slim cigarette and lit up.

'It's a new one,' he turned to me in a tone of confidentiality. 'It's one of these Chubb's Bankers' safes; steel plates throughout, body plates one inch thick, door plates one and a quarter inches with ten working bolts securing the door and engaging all four sides of the door to the frame. Diagonal bolts, too, which makes things harder. Two locks, as well. I hadn't even got anywhere with the first lock, let alone the second one, and then you popped your head round the door! I really must visit Chubbs in St James's and look a little more closely at their new safe designs.'

The shock of seeing Raffles alive after I believed him to be four years dead was, thanks to a second glass of brandy, beginning to wear off.

I opened my mouth to demand an explanation but Raffles silenced me with a gesture of a begloved hand.

'Just a second, Bunny, old fellow. As you can see, I'm alive and relatively well, so let's skip that part for a bit. What I want to know is what you are doing here? This place belongs to Lord Toby Devenish, doesn't it? And according to my intelligence, no one is supposed to be at home tonight. Lord Toby is off to some soirée, his servants have the night off and there is only one caretaker, a rather deaf old man who sleeps over the stables at the back of the house.'

I stifled a million questions which were flooding into my mind.

'Look here, Raffles . . .' I began.

'It's rather important that I know what I'm up against, Bunny,' he pressed in an earnest voice.

'Well,' I said begrudgingly, 'the house does belong to Lord Toby. Toby Devenish happens to be my brother-in-law.'

Raffles face broke into a grin.

'What ho!' he exclaimed. 'So you've married at last, Bunny? Congratulations! Do I know the lady? Devenish, eh? Devenish . . .'

'I should say you do know her,' I cried hotly.

He frowned again.

'Oh Lor',' he said. 'Alice Devenish, of course. I should have guessed.'

'The one woman who saw through you, Raffles,' I said,

10

not without a certain amount of malice and pride. 'The one woman who guessed that the notorious amateur cracksman and you were one and the same. Even so she never betrayed you nor me.'*

'So you and Alice Devenish are married?' he mused. Knowing him so well I must confess that his usual bland countenance was somewhat shaken.

'After you were kil. . . after *I thought* you were killed at Mafeking, I led the troop out of the Boer ambush but was hit in the leg. It's given me a bit of a stiff knee. When I came back to England, Alice was waiting for me. She encouraged me to take up an honest life again and live down my past misdemeanours. We were married two years ago.'

Raffles annoyed me somewhat by receiving my recital with a somewhat cynical grin.

'Poor old chap. Captured by a good woman,' he murmured. 'And just what do you do with your life nowadays?'

'You know I used to write the occasional article and story? Well, I have had a moderate success in that field.'

Raffles abruptly frowned and glanced towards the ceiling.

'And where is the admirable Mrs Manders now?'

'Alice has gone to visit friends in Paris. I had some business appointments in London and could not go with her.'

'And do you usually stay with your brother-in-law?'

'No,' I returned, shaking my head. 'I usually live down in Bosham, near Chichester in Sussex. I only come to town now and then to visit editors and so forth. It was deuce lonely with Alice away and so I caught an early train up to town this morning . . . yesterday morning,' I corrected myself, glancing at the study clock. 'I chose the wrong day to socialise because Devenish was off to one of his damnable parties, you know the sort of Bohemian thing he loves, and it was the servants day off. I just curled myself up with a book, fell asleep and the next thing was . . .'

* See 'The Last Word' recorded in *A Thief in the Night*, 1905.

'The next thing,' interrupted Raffles, 'was my untimely arrival.'

He sat back and gave me a long examination.

'Dear old Bunny,' he murmured. 'Just like the old days, eh?'

I could not suppress a shiver.

'Except, Raffles,' I said, trying to give some force to my voice, 'you are the burglar while I stand *in loco parentis* for the owner of this house.'

'Indeed you do,' he returned, clapping me on the knee. 'I forgot. But, and importantly, when can we expect the arrival of the owner?'

'He doesn't usually get in much before four o'clock after these soirées.'

'Ah,' Raffles became solemn, 'and since you have caught me, dear Bunny, are you holding me until he comes or shall you contact the police immediately?'

'Dash it, Raffles,' I cried in agitation, 'I hadn't thought . . . don't be so deuced unfair to a chap! Of course I'm not holding you. Look, for the sake of our friendship, I won't say a word.'

He seized my hand and pumped it.

'Well, well, Bunny, I do believe that you are not gone beyond recall.'

I was perplexed and said so.

'I mean that the delectable Mrs Manders has not completely captured your soul . . . a little larceny still lurks there, eh? A little taste for adventure?'

'Oh stop that rot, Raffles. I'm respectable now and I darn well think you owe me an explanation.'

Raffles sprang to his feet like an exuberant schoolboy.

'An explanation it shall be, Bunny old friend. But help me pack away my tools in case Lord Toby comes in and surprises us. Here, hand me that jemmy.'

Automatically I handed him the jemmy. It was as if the years had dropped away and we two were working together once more. I was piqued to the quick for all my horror of the situation.

'Now tell me what has happened to you, Raffles,' I

demanded, after he had packed the terrible tools of his profession into a small Gladstone bag.

'Certainly, Bunny. Pour me another tot of that brandy.'

While I did so he flourished his cigarette case.

'Care for a Sullivan? They are getting deuced hard to get since the war.'

I shook my head.

'Right, old chap. Now, where shall I begin?'

'May, 1900,' I returned immediately. 'The Boers were besieging Mafeking to try to capture its important railway yards. Our garrison there – I think Baden-Powell was in command – was still holding out after six months of siege warfare. Our troop was, as you recall, in the vanguard of the relief column and we were ordered to probe the Boer's encirclement to see if we could fight our way into the town and raise the siege.'

Raffles nodded reflectively.

'I remember,' and then with a touch of irony, 'I *was* the captain of the troop, Bunny.'

He paused a while and then as he did not commence his narrative I prompted:

'We were ambushed by a Boer commando and you fell in the first fusillade. I tried to help you but the sergeant said you were dead and we were forced to retreat. A few weeks later, May 17 I think it was, the siege was actually raised and you were officially reported dead in the casualty lists. Within a couple of days I was already on my way back to England in a hospital ship.'

Raffles drew deeply on his cigarette.

'Well, old fellow,' he said finally, 'as you can observe yourself, I was not killed. Mind you, it was a nasty wound. The bullet passed through my shoulder and when I regained consciousness I was in a makeshift Boer hospital. Not only that but while I had lain unconscious someone had looted my belongings, including all my identification. The Boers were not such bad fellows, a bit prim and puritanical, I'll grant you. But on the whole they were pretty decent. I was well nursed and one day even Piet Joubert, the Boer general, came to see if we wounded prisoners were being well treated.'

'*General* Joubert?' I asked incredulously. 'The Boer commander-in-chief?'

'The same,' affirmed Raffles. 'Well, the first thing the Boers asked me was what my name, rank and number were. It suddenly occurred to me that the war might be over soon and a dead A. J. Raffles might have some distinct advantages over a live one. While I lay working it out, I pretended I couldn't remember much.

'Within a few days we withdrew from Kimberley, where they had taken me, and indeed, the withdrawal became a rout out of Natal towards the Transvaal. We prisoners were taken to Paardenberg. But the British troops were cutting through the Boers like a knife through butter.

'I now discovered that the looter who had stolen my papers was blown up by an artillery shell. The newspapers printed my name as being killed in action. That convinced me to leave poor A. J. Raffles dead and let Private Arthur Roberts emerge. That was the name I gave the Boers, anyway.'

'But . . . but didn't you think what I must have felt, believing you to be dead?' I demanded at his easy deception. 'Why, for the past four years I . . .'

There was a catch in my throat which I could not well disguise.

Raffles laid a hand on my shoulder.

'Dear old Bunny. You were the best and closest of friends. I only regret my deception because of your suffering. Still, at the time I thought – perhaps Bunny would be better off without a Raffles to mislead him. Wasn't I right? Here you are, a man of means, happily married, and all within a few years of my unseemly death.'

I blew my nose loudly.

'That's not the beastly point, Raffles,' I choked.

'Anyway,' he continued, 'I was a prisoner of the Boers for over a year or so. I rather enjoyed myself. No worries. We prisoners used to play some passable cricket to while away the time. Anyway, Kronje eventually surrendered the Paardenberg garrison on the banks of the Modder

14

River to Kitchener. The Boers were now a disorderly crowd of terrified men fleeing before the British.

'The whole place was in an uproar. The war being over, I decided that my country no longer needed me. I took what few possessions that I had, requisitioned a horse from a rather disgruntled Boer, and pressed off northwards. Needless to say, I was not listed as a deserter because there was no such person as Arthur Roberts and A. J. Raffles was dead, killed in the execution of a brief but meritorious service.'

I sat back and looked at Raffles in amazement.

'But the surrender of the Boers and the signing of the peace treaty at Vereeniging was two years ago. What have you been up to since then?'

Raffles grinned.

'Having quite an adventurous life, old top. I made my way up to British East Africa and settled for a while in Nairobi. I suddenly found myself involved in some colonial wars. Old Sir Donald Stewart was governor of the territory and he was having trouble with some natives, the Nandi. The Nandi were resisting the *pax Britannia*, scampering down to ambush small groups of settlers and trying to destroy our rail links to the western part of the Kenyan highlands. They weren't much of an army but they were a jolly sore thorn in the colonial administration's flesh. I spent a year chasing them.'

'And then?'

Raffles stretched his legs and took out another cigarette. He gazed at it reflectively, pulled a face and replaced it in his silver case.

'Nasty habit, really,' he said. 'My doctor tells me it's not wholly good for one but then none of the pleasures of life really are, eh?'

'What then?' I pressed.

'Then, dear Bunny, with some money in my pocket for a year's service in the British East African Police, as they called the unit I was involved with, and some money accrued from a few deals on the side, Arthur Roberts returned to England, home and beauty. I arrived in London four weeks ago.'

'And immediately took up life where you left it?' I said bitterly.

'Old habits die hard, Bunny,' agreed Raffles blandly. 'Yes, they do die hard and I have a certain standard of living which I feel I must upkeep.'

I stood up and paced the room with some agitation.

'Why didn't you contact me immediately?' I demanded. 'Surely you could trust me. I could get you work or . . .'

'Work?' The word was like a pistol shot. Raffles gazed at me in disapproval. 'With due respect, old fellow, you don't expect me to start work at my time of life? It's not work I want, nor is it really the money . . .'

'Then why?' I asked in perplexity, motioning towards the safe.

'Surely, Bunny, you can recall the thrill of adventure, the coursing of your blood in excitement?'

Raffles could never understand the fact that I did not wholeheartedly enter into the enjoyment of his profession.

'But Raffles . . .'

He suddenly jerked up a hand for silence and adopted the pose of one listening.

A shrill whining sound came to our ears which stopped before the house.

'What's that?'

I moved uneasily.

'That's Devenish's carriage.'

'His carriage?' frowned Raffles.

'Yes. He's got one of those Electric Broughams.'

'Ah, I forgot all about those infernal machines. Well, I must be on my way, Bunny. You'll not say a word about seeing me, eh?'

He bent and picked up his bag, making for the study window.

'Lights out now, Bunny.'

My hand went like ice as I heard the fumbling of a key in the front door.

I flicked off the electric light switch and plunged the study into darkness.

The dark shadow of Raffles paused at the open window, half sitting on the sill.

'Come and see me for tea in my rooms, Bunny, there's a good chap. We can continue this talk then.'

I sighed in frustration but nodded in obedience.

'Wait!' I called in a desperate whisper as the figure began to dissolve into the darkness of the night. 'Where are your rooms?'

A low chuckle answered me.

'At Albany, of course. You'll find me there under Arthur Roberts.'

I opened my mouth.

'Don't worry,' interrupted the voice, 'no one there recognises me after all these years. At tea-time, then.'

I could hear the front door opening so I bent quickly and drew down the window and secured the blinds. I was halfway to the door when it was thrown open and the light flashed on leaving me standing, a sorry spectacle no doubt, blinking in its bright glare.

'Good God, Harry! What are you doing creeping around in the dark?'

Lord Toby Devenish, my brother-in-law, stood swaying slightly in the doorway, still holding the switch in one hand. He was a tall, fair haired man, with a transparent white skin which, at that moment, was somewhat blotched by drink. His blue eyes seemed to have difficulty in focussing on me. And his voice was slurred.

'Hello, Toby,' I answered sheepishly. 'I just had a drink out of your decanter.'

Devenish came unsteadily into the room and sniffed.

'And a few cigarettes as well,' he added, observing the stale air. 'I didn't know you smoked.'

I glanced quickly at him but there was no suspicion in his voice.

'Well, I'll be off back to bed. Er, um, 'night, Toby.'

Devenish grinned, one hand clasping the decanter which he half raised as if in a wave.

' 'Night, Harry, old boy.'

I retraced my steps to the warm bed I had left an hour before to find it cold and inhospitable. I found it impossible to sleep until dawn found me falling into an uneasy slumber of exhaustion.

Henry Manders, came that nasal treble of my conscience. Henry Manders! You will not go to Albany. It means nothing but trouble.

The obnoxious treble was the last thing that registered before I fell asleep.

CHAPTER THREE

It was with a feeling of forboding that I turned along Piccadilly and halted outside of Albany at four-fifteen that day. I had risen late that morning with a beastly headache as if I had drunk the best part of two quarts of champagne on the previous evening. But the cause of my headache was no hangover. My mind was constantly revolving about the return of Raffles and its possible effects on my now staid and sober life. Lord Toby had departed for his club by the time I entered the breakfast room and commenced to toy with my toast and devilled kidneys. I tried to scan the columns of *The Times* but could not concentrate. I did not even attempt to examine the *Sporting Record*. Finally, my mind filled with gloomy thoughts, I made my way to the Hammam in Jermyn Street. I have always regarded a turkish bath as a refuge, an asylum, from the cares of the world. I entered and went upstairs to the changing rooms where a Chinese functionary took my clothes and handed me a towel. Then I stepped into the steamy bathroom and tried to let my mind go blank. It refused to do so.

Thus it was with a strange feeling of apprehension I eventually entered the familiar portals of Albany and asked at the caretaker's office for the rooms of Mister Arthur Roberts. I nearly made a *faux pas* by asking for A. J. Raffles; the name, in that place, tripping so easily off my tongue. The porter asked my name and, lifting a telephone receiver, dialled a number. 'Mister Manders to see you, sir.' A pause. 'Very good, sir.' The porter pointed to a lift and, to my astonishment, gave me the number of Raffles' old suite of rooms. It was all too uncomfortably familiar.

Albany was a splendid place, an elegant place, whose courtyard and high walls were bounded by Piccadilly and Vigo Street, sheltering its inhabitants from the hustle and bustle of the rail services which terminated at Piccadilly Station a few yards away. I have never ceased to marvel over the old worldliness of Albany. In the days of James II, Lord Sutherland owned a house on the site which was knocked down in 1804 to make way for a new edifice consecrated to the memory of the Duke of York and Albany and designated as rooms or apartments for bachelors of good reputation. It was a use which had not been altered during its hundred years of occupation. Lord Byron once occupied rooms here. So did Macauley, Henry Luttrell and Bulwer Lytton. Raffles' own suite, which faced out onto the Albany courtyard, was once the home of the eccentric Matthew Lewis, the writer of such fantasies as *The Monk* and *Castle Spectre*. He became a Member of Parliament, as I recall.

Raffles had the door open as I entered the corridor and beckoned me inside.

'Come in, Bunny, old fellow. Come in.'

Raffles led the way in and sprawled on a velvet-covered chaise-longue. He leant back and smiled. The same old Raffles. I see his indolent athletic figure, his pale, sharp, clean-shaven features; his curly black hair now tinged with silver strands; his strong unscrupulous mouth. I shuddered in the beam of his eyes, cold and luminous as stars, shining into the innermost recesses of my brain, sifting the very secrets of my heart.

I turn my gaze to the old familiar walls with their decorations and furnishings. It was as if the years had never intervened since the last time I stood there.

Raffles had always done himself well in his style of furnishing. Aubusson carpets covered his floors and the oak panelled walls were inlaid with *toile de jouie*. His chairs, chaise-longue and escritoire were of *Louis Quinze* satinwood while, in a corner, stood a Buhl cabinet in which Raffles had a superb collection of Dresden and Sèvres. In another cabinet stood a dignified collection of Waterford cut-glass. Colour prints after Fragonard hung strategically and there were several original pre-Raphaelite paintings, a school Raffles was especially fond of. There was a Rossetti, a work by Ford Maddox Brown and some prints by Morris and Burne-Jones. It was a room I knew well. Yet how had Raffles managed to keep these rooms, if the Albany management thought him dead?

'Well, Bunny?' drawled Raffles. 'Shall you pour or shall I?'

He motioned towards the silver tea tray which had been laid on a side table with plates of hot muffins and cakes.

I motioned him to pour and gazed curiously round the room.

'How did you manage to keep this on, Raffles?'

He shrugged deprecatingly.

'I always kept on the suite, Bunny. I paid the Albany trustees by banker's order.'

'But if Raffles is officially dead how then . . .?'

'Simplicity itself,' smiled Raffles. 'When I decided on my new identity, I simply wrote the trustees a letter which I posted in Chai-Chai . . .'

'Chai-Chai?'

'On the Limpopo River in Portuguese East Africa. I sent a letter which I dated before my sad demise in South Africa. The letter simply gave instructions to my bank that, in the event of my death in the South African war, my cousin Arthur Roberts would be sole beneficiary of my estate. The estate was to pay the rental for my rooms until such time as Mr Roberts made alternative arrangements. When Mr Roberts arrived in London a month ago he claimed the estates and also made application to the trustees and secretary of Albany to take over the rooms of the late lamented Mr Raffles. The secretary gravely informed Mr Roberts that, after due consideration, the trustees would allow Mr Roberts to occupy Mr Raffles' rooms.'

'But is it safe?' I ventured. 'Won't people recognise you?'

'Bunny, old top, you'd be surprised at how trusting people are. Most people take your word that you are who you claim to be. However, as Mr Roberts is a cousin of the late Mr Raffles, any resemblance can be explained away.'

I shook my head slowly.

'And so . . . .?' I prompted.

'And so, Bunny, you see me short of cash once more and plying the old, honourable profession.'

'I thought you said last night you were doing it for the thrill of adventure and not the cash?' I sneered.

'So I am, old thing, but cash is a great incentive.'

'If it's cash you want, I could make you a loan,' I said.

Raffles leant back and held up both hands, an expression of mock horror on his handsome face.

'Spare my days, old thing! I haven't fallen that low yet.'

'Yet low enough to break into Toby Devenish's place last night,' I retorted.

'Oh, come now,' he chided, a hint of sarcasm in his voice. 'Time was when you did not think such activities were "low" . . . Bunny, I swear you've grown into a pious rabbit in your dotage. Is it marriage?'

I bridled immediately.

'One grows up,' I snapped, hating his pun on my nickname.

Raffles arched his eyebrows and pulled a face.

'Do you recall the *Ides of March*, Bunny?' he suddenly mused.

For the moment I frowned, wondering why he had suddenly switched the conversation.

'Do you remember the night you came to me here, in this very room, and confessed that you had been writing dud cheques to cover your losses at baccarat and that you were in a desperate situation?'

I stirred uncomfortably as the memory came like a sharp needle in my conscience.

'You remember,' went on Raffles remorselessly, 'how

you were so moved with despair at the prospect of ruin and dishonour that you were finally determined to end your miserable existence? You pulled forth a revolver and were going to blast your brains out with it.' He gave a slightly sour smile at my reddening cheeks. 'It was rather despicable to involve another in one's own destruction, Bunny,' he admonished. 'Perhaps that was a miserable appeal to your baser egoism?'

'Well,' I replied hotly, 'a fat lot you cared about whether I emptied my brains on your carpet or not. I believe you wanted me to carry out the deed.'

Raffles chuckled.

'Not quite, old fellow. I did rather want to see if you had spunk enough to do it. Still, enough of that.'

He gave one of his damnably disarming smiles, having made his point and making me feel rather ridiculous at my self-righteousness.

'I'll be honest, Bunny. In spite of what I said last night, the fact remains that I am quite stoney broke. I haven't a bean. My bank is starting to get agitated. I must do a job or go under.'

'But dash it, Raffles, I told you that I could give you a loan . . .'

He waved his hand in dismissal.

'Time was, Bunny, that you would have jumped at a chance to collect some tax free money.'

'Times have changed,' I said decisively.

'Have they, old chap?' His grey eyes stared straight into mine, making me feel naked. 'Don't you feel a longing for adventure, the quickening of your pulse, the excitement and financial reward?'

Damn it! The man could read me like a book. True, that in my new life I did look back with a curious longing on those gay, adventurous days when Raffles and I were celebrated, in anonymity, of course, as the most daring cracksmen of the age. It was not the financial rewards; no, it was the adventure and excitement which I looked back on with nostalgia. I am not a brave sort of chap; I have never made out otherwise. But there had been a certain stimulus which our adventures had brought me and which I missed. I saw Raffles smiling mockingly at me and pulled myself together.

'I am having quite a success in my writing,' I said lamely. 'That's excitement enough.'

His mouth quirked.

He glanced abruptly at the Dresden china clock, it was nearly seven-thirty.

'Tell you what, Bunny. I'll stand you dinner at a little restaurant I know in North London.'

'You've just said that you were without funds,' I pointed out.

He smiled disarmingly.

'It's one of the few places my credit is still good.'

In spite of some uneasiness I agreed to join him and we went downstairs and hailed a Hansom cab. Raffles gave the man an address in St Johns Wood and then fell to reminiscing about the war in South Africa and his subsequent experiences as a prisoner-of-war. It was twilight when we alighted at a spot not far from the main thoroughfare of the Finchley Road. Raffles paid off the cabby while I peered around searching for the restaurant.

'Where is this place, Raffles?' said I, not seeing anything remotely resembling an eating house among the sedate suburban mansions.

'This way, old chap,' murmured Raffles and proceeded to walk along a side road. After ten minutes we stopped on a street corner, in the shadow of a tall tree.

Raffles nodded towards a large house set well back in its own grounds and which was shrouded in darkness.

'See that house, Bunny?'

I nodded wondering what he was up to.

'That's the house of Sir Emanuel Rose.'

Everyone knew of Sir Emanuel Rose, banker and entrepreneur.

A cold feeling began to tingle in my spine, a feeling that I had not experienced for many years.

'Shall I tell you something about Sir Emanuel?'

I did not reply but Raffles went on heedless of his unanswered question.

'Rose was a crony of the financier and diamond

23

magnate Sir Abe Bailey. They were behind the Jameson Raid into the Transvaal Republic which was the spark which caused the Boer War. Remember? Jameson and his men raided the Transvaal and tried to get the British settlers to rise up against the Boers. It was a blatant act of provocation and, of course, the Boers were provoked. Big financiers like Bailey and Rose wanted the war knowing full well the tiny Boer republic would be overcome by force. Then they could step in and take over the gold and diamond mines of the Transvaal. Men like Sir Emanuel are responsible for the deaths of thousands of men, women and children who perished in that war.'

'So?' I demanded, an edge to my voice.

'Sir Emanuel is the perfect candidate for being relieved of some of his ill-gotten gains. He had a very nice collection of antique snuff boxes which I have a buyer for.'

I stared at Raffles in indignation.

'So it was a ruse! Your invitation to dinner was nothing more than a downright . . .'

He stilled me with an upraised hand.

'Not so, Bunny. There is a little restaurant hard by Swiss Cottage a short walk from here. It is fully my intention to go there after I have helped Sir Emanuel with a more even distribution of his wealth.'

'Raffles,' I breathed, 'you *are* a bounder!'

Raffles grinned.

'You are probably right, old thing.'

He glanced across at the house.

'Now, old top, I did plan to crack this crib myself but it would be an immense aid if I had a partner.'

I started to protest vehemently.

'You see,' he went on, 'I've made sure that Sir Emanuel is away in the country and that his servants have gone with him. So the house is empty. It would be like taking sweets from a small child, as our American cousins say. But two men are better than one to carry away the plunder. What say you, Bunny? Just help me this once, for old time's sake. Nothing could be safer, or easier, and you'll wind up with a few thousand in your pocket before midnight.'

24

I opened my mouth to admonish him but he shrugged.

'Of course, I'll understand if you say no. I know the burdens that marriage and respectability place on one. I'll understand if you want to wait here or walk on to the restaurant. It's your decision, old chap.'

Oh his cleverness! His fiendish cleverness! Had he fallen back on threats, coercion, sneers, all might have been different even then. But he set me free to leave him in the lurch. He would not blame me. He did not even bind me to secrecy; he trusted me. He knew my weakness and my strength and was playing on both with his master's touch.

'This once, Raffles,' I said grimly after a deep struggle.

His face broadened into a smile and he stretched out his hand.

'Well done, Bunny, old chap. Why, it will be like the old days. Come now, sharp's the word!'

My feeling of apprehension was replaced by a more curious sensation as I followed him towards the darkened house. The rapid beating of my heart echoed the pant of my breath as the excitement sent my blood surging into my extremities.

A dog was barking in the distance as Raffles and I paused outside a side gate which gave ingress through a tall hedge. He glanced about in the gloom before swinging the gate open noiselessly and motioning me through. I pushed my fears into the back of my mind, realising – guiltily – that I was enjoying myself for the first time in some years. In fact, it seemed that there had hardly been an interval at all since my last nocturnal trip with Raffles; all that he had taught me came back as second nature as we slipped across the gloomy shadows of the lawn and made our way to the side of the house.

Raffles produced a small pocket torch.

'I've been studying the place for a few days,' he whispered reassuringly, as he bent to the lock of the french windows and started to pick at it with a slim clasp knife. 'This leads into the study. Above the desk is a portrait of Sir Emanuel and behind that is an old wall safe. Nothing could be more simple . . . ah, that's it.'

There was a click and Raffles swung the french window open and stepped cautiously in. I followed, closing the window behind me. For a few moments we stood there, by the windows, while Raffles probed the room with his torch.

'There's the portrait,' I said.

'Splendid!'

He stepped quietly across the room, reached up and removed the picture from the wall. Its removal revealed an elderly looking wall safe of a type I had seen Raffles open many times.

I stood silently while he bent an ear to the safe, his fingers dexterously twisting the dial, as he played with the combination. It seemed only a moment before there came a tell-tale click and, with a sigh, Raffles swung the safe door open. From the pocket of his overcoat, he produced a small black cloth sack.

'Hold this a moment, Bunny,' he ordered, and, as I did so, he shone his torch into the interior of the safe. 'Great stuff!' he chortled, his arm reaching in and coming out with a tiny golden object in his fingers. In the light of his torch I beheld a small bejewelled box. He dropped it into the sack and soon several other similar objects had followed it.

'Stand still! The game is up!'

The raucous voice echoing in the room froze me to the spot. Suddenly the lights blazed on and the french windows and the door seemed to spew forth policemen.

Raffles swung round open-mouthed. Even in my petrified state I observed that he had an expression of utter astonishment on his usually well-controlled features.

A heavy, red-faced man in an ulster and bowler hat came up and stood, hands on hip, grinning in triumph at us.

'Well, well, well. *Mister* Raffles and *Mister* Manders. At long, long last I've finally got the goods on you!'

There was no mistaking the Scottish burr in his voice. I nearly passed out in my agitation as I met the malignant

26

gaze of our old arch-enemy – Inspector Mackenzie of Scotland Yard.

CHAPTER FOUR

Raffles was the first to recover himself. He gave a little shrug of resignation.

'I believe the expression is "it's a fair cop, guv'nor",' he said evenly. 'I must confess, however, I am surprised to see you here, inspector.'

Mackenzie grinned nastily.

'Detective Chief Superintendent Mackenzie now, *Mister* Raffles,' he said, throwing out his chest importantly.

Raffles nodded absently.

'A well deserved promotion, it seems,' he dryly commented. 'Your powers of detection have made a remarkable improvement since the old days.'

Mackenzie reddened at the thrust.

'There's nothing miraculous about me preventing this little caper. You should learn to choose your fence with more care. He recognised you and realised that I would be more than interested in meeting up with you in spite of the lapse of years. He owed me a favour and has repaid me handsomely.'

I saw a look of understanding momentarily flash across Raffles' face but he had composed his features within a second.

'So my friendly "broker" grassed on me? That explains it.'

Mackenzie now turned his malevolent attention to me, shaking his head sadly.

'Well now, Mister Manders; I must say I didn't bargain on meeting you. I've kept an eye on you these last few years and thought you were going straight. Still, once a thief . . .'

'He is going straight,' interrupted Raffles. 'Bunny is

straight as a die, Mackenzie. I tricked him into accompanying me here tonight.'

I felt a warm feeling for Raffles. At least he stood by a chum.

Mackenzie laughed coarsely.

'You can tell all that to the judge.'

He waved to the uniformed constables who came forward and removed the sack of snuff boxes and – horrors! – placed handcuffs upon Raffles and me. We were whisked off to a police van and before I knew it were being ushered through the portals of New Scotland Yard. There we were separated. I was taken to a small, drab cell, where all my clothes were removed and, in return, I was given a coarse prison suit to put on. Then, without so much as a word to me, the constables went out and the iron door clanged shut on my despair.

It is almost impossible to describe the feelings that passed through me during those lonely hours spent in that bleak cell with its one coat of green wash paint barely disguising its damp, crumbling brick walls. At first I paced the room banging my hands in agitation and cursing Raffles volubly for the folly in which he had led me. Next I cursed myself for my own stupidity and weakness. I had always been easily led. Then I cursed Mackenzie, always our implacable enemy, for his final triumph. Finally, I was overcome by shame and dread for soon the news of the arrest of the celebrated Raffles and his partner, Manders, would be plastered over every European newspaper. What would my beloved Alice say? Dear Alice, who had tried so hard to reform my weak and worthless character? I broke out into a cold sweat. Oh, the very shame of it!

So overcome with shame and remorse was I that at one time I contemplated suicide; yes, suicide! My contemplation even went to the point where I examined the bars of my cell and looked at the feasibility of using the thin, fraying prison shirt as a substitute rope to tie around my neck and the bars. However, I was not entirely despairing when I discovered the feat to be an impossibility.

I almost lost track of time for, strangely, no one came to

see me after a few preliminary questions and my only contact with the outside world was the gaoler who brought my meals.

A full twenty-four hours must surely have passed when I began to feel an aggression welling within me. I knew my rights as a citizen and surely I was entitled to consult a solicitor to plead my case? Surely, the police should charge me and not leave me to rot in solitary confinement? I had barely made up my mind to make my demands known when the cell door opened with a rattling of keys and two burly constables entered bearing my clothes. I was given a brusque instruction to put them on.

I had just tied and straightened my neck-tie when they whisked me from the cell. We hurried along a maze of passage ways and then out through a door in the street. It turned out to be a side door of the New Scotland Yard building. A group of inquisitive street urchins were standing by the entrance and immediately set to booing as I was hustled out. Oh, the very shame of it! What would Alice say?

Within the instant I found myself bundled into the back of a police van, the two constables following. They sat on either side of me with wooden expressions, never exchanging one word. The driver cracked his whip and the van trundled forward across the cobbles.

'Are we going to a magistrate's court?' I demanded, after we had left Whitehall, turned round Trafalgar Square and started to proceed up the Charing Cross Road at a fairly steady trot.

One of the policemen regarded me with some amusement.

'At this time of night?' he mocked.

I saw his point at once. It must have been about eight o'clock in the evening and there was a hint of dusk gathering. Certainly no magistrate would sit at such an hour.

'Where am I being taken to?' I persisted.

'You'll soon find out,' replied the same policeman and then fell to examining his fingernails with an air of distaste.

It was quite some time before the police van rattled into the drive of a tall house which I had observed to be situated in Fitzjohn's Avenue in Hampstead. I was frankly puzzled by our destination for the police van had made several detours and circled back on itself three times. Frankly, I had begun to wonder whether I was being taken for a ride simply in order to give the police horses some exercise.

I had hardly descended from the van when a second police van came into the courtyard and Raffles himself was unceremoniously deposited on the cobbles.

With a glad cry I made towards him but the constables held me back.

'No talking now!' said the loquacious policeman.

Raffles shot me an encouraging smile from a worried, pale face.

We were propelled through a side door and along a dimly lit corridor. At a broad wooden door we were halted and a constable tapped gently upon it. It was opened immediately and the face of Mackenzie regarded us dourly.

'Thanks vera much, constables,' he said with a dismissing wave of his hand. Then to us: 'Come along in, laddies, and mind ye be on ye're best behaviour.'

The room was dimly lit with one lamp only on the corner of a desk which stood at the far end of the room. The furnishings, or what I could see of them, were warm and comfortable. It was clearly a working study, lined from floor to ceiling with masses of old books. There were two empty chairs placed before the desk and some other seats and a couch placed at strategic points around the room.

Mackenzie ushered us forward and closed the door behind us, taking a stand with his back to the door. Raffles caught my eye and merely raised an eyebrow to show his bewilderment.

Seated at the desk was a big man of about fifty years of age. He had a bull-like neck bursting from his spotless white collar and tie. Above it an aggressive jawline thrust out in challenge. His face was very familiar and I racked

30

my brains to try to remember where I had seen him before.

At the same time I also became aware of two figures on the opposite side of the room but the lamp was so placed that they stood completely in shadows.

The man at the desk sat back and stared for a long while at my companion and barely spared me a casual glance.

'So you are A. J. Raffles?' he murmured at last.

I immediately placed the soft modulated accent as that of a cultured Irishman; moreover, for I am not without talent at spotting accents, I deduced the man was from Dublin or its environs.

Raffles gave a half bow towards the man.

'I am he,' he answered gravely, as if introducing himself to his host at some dinner party.

'And do you know me, Mister Raffles?' the big man asked quietly.

I saw Raffles' mouth quirk in a smile.

'You are Edward Henry Carson, Member of Parliament for the Dublin University constituency and Solicitor-General of the United Kingdom.'

I gasped.

So that was where I had seen the big man before – in pictures in the popular newspapers and periodicals!

Carson seemed satisfied with the effect his name had on me though I must point out that it did not appear to have overly impressed Raffles.

'Be seated, Mister Raffles. You, too, Mister Manders,' said the Solicitor-General motioning at the chairs before his desk. 'You are, perhaps, wondering why you are here?'

I nodded eagerly but Raffles answered in a drawl, as if bored by the proceedings: 'I presume we shall be told that in your own good time.'

Carson's face wreathed in a smile.

'You really must allow His Majesty's Government to have its little theatrics, Mister Raffles. After all, you are not particularly against indulging in them yourself.'

Raffles inclined his head as if to say 'touché!'

'In fact, Mister Raffles, when I have told you the story

31

which is the cause of you being here you will probably appreciate this secret rendezvous.'

There was a silence during which the Solicitor-General picked up a paper knife and began to tap it against the desk top.

He was interrupted by a hollow cough from one of the men sitting in the shadows. The Solicitor-General glanced up like a small boy caught doing something he should not.

'It is hard to know where to begin . . .' he said, suddenly embarrassed.

I had become piqued to the quick by this drama.

'Chief Superintendent Mackenzie informs me that you are regarded by Scotland Yard as one of the best safe-breakers in the country.'

Raffles gave a modest laugh.

'An amateur cracksman, if you please, sir. And, since I am so far committed, for the sake of accuracy let me add that I am not one of the best but, indeed, *the* best.'

I heard Mackenzie smothering a burst of indignation in a fit of coughing.

The Solicitor-General had a twinkle in his eye.

'Quite so, Mister Raffles. Well, to be blunt, His Majesty's Government has a need to employ a . . . an amateur cracksman.'

Raffles' demeanour did not change but I noticed he sat straighter in his chair. As for myself, my mouth was fairly agape.

'How do you feel about such a proposition, Mister Raffles?' pressed the Solicitor-General.

'It would depend on the deal, as our American cousins say, sir,' Raffles answered readily.

'Quite so,' murmured the Solicitor-General looking towards the men sitting in the shadows.

There was another pause.

'Mister Raffles – Mister Manders: over the past years you have both displayed a talent which is fairly unique. You have succeeded in opening safes and strong rooms which were claimed to be burglar proof. For years you thwarted the best brains,' here he gave a withering glance in Mackenzie's direction, 'the best brains at Scotland Yard. In fact your activities became a national disgrace and there would have been nothing I would have liked better than to put you both behind bars.' He paused and smiled. 'That is until a few days ago.'

He looked down at the paper knife he had been holding as if observing it for the first time.

'As you say, Mister Raffles, you are unquestionably the best cracksman in the country.'

Raffles gave an ironic half bow from his chair.

'We now find it of vital national interest to employ a man of your not inconsiderable talent. We have also noted that you have both displayed a national zeal during the late conflict in South Africa, even though you, Mister Raffles, decided to discharge yourself rather than wait for a grateful government to do so with the addition of a Distinguished Service Cross which, as you know, was awarded posthumously after Mafeking.'

For the first time I saw Raffles look a trifle uncomfortable.

'But that's in the past, gentlemen,' went on the Solicitor-General. 'We approach you not just because of your remarkable talents but because you have shown, at times, that you are possessed of a patriotic spirit . . .'

'Excuse me, Mister Solicitor-General,' interrupted Raffles softly, 'but I take it that you will be coming to the point soon?'

The Solicitor-General drew his brows together and coughed irritably as if unused to anyone daring to interrupt him when in full flow.

'Quite so,' he said dryly. 'The point, gentlemen, is this: we are prepared to wipe the slate clean, to grant you a free pardon for any transgressions committed in the past. In return for that pardon we wish you to complete a simple job on behalf of the government.'

The offer drove the breath from my body.

Not so Raffles for he languidly stretched out his legs.

'As you are asking us, men whom our friend Mackenzie here has sworn to put away for life on more than one occasion, and as the reward must be considered considerable by His Majesty's Government, I presume the job is not really that simple?' he said, sarcasm edging his voice.

The Solicitor-General once more glanced towards the figures in the shadows.

'I can say without hesitation that it is a fairly simple job for someone with your talents. You will be required to open a safe, take out a package of papers and bring them to me without the owner of the safe knowing or capturing you.'

'And where would this safe be situated?' pressed Raffles dubiously.

'Here, in London.'

I turned to Raffles.

'Well, I for one am in agreement. What can we lose? We are in such a beastly mess that I don't think we have an option.'

Raffles grimaced.

'That point, what can we lose, is precisely what I am trying to discover, Bunny, old chap,' he said quietly. 'Perhaps we can lose our lives?'

Mackenzie moved forward.

'Och, I knew it was no use to argue wi' the likes o' these, sir. Best let me take them back to the Yard.'

The Solicitor-General stayed him with an upraised hand.

'Not yet, Mackenzie. I can appreciate Mister Raffles wants as much information as he can before making a decision. Unfortunately, Mister Raffles, I cannot offer that information until some agreement has been reached.'

Raffles suddenly stood up.

'In that case, gentlemen, I shall make *you* an offer.'

I looked at him astounded by his audacity.

'Bunny . . . Mister Manders and I will undertake your job on the following conditions: in addition to the free pardon for both of us, you will meet all out of pocket expenses involved in the job and the sum of one thousand pounds sterling apiece will be payable as a fee on completion of the job.'

Mackenzie was spluttering in inarticulate rage.

34

The Solicitor-General frowned and shot yet another look towards the shadows. Then he smiled and nodded.

'Very well, Mister Raffles – and you, Mister Manders. We have an agreement.'

Raffles nodded and then turned to the figures in the shadows.

'And now, sir, perhaps you will introduce us to your superior . . .?'

A small man in his mid-fifties rose from the couch in the shadows and stepped forward into the circle of light. I paled. I had no difficulty in recognising Arthur James Balfour, the Prime Minister of the United Kingdom of Great Britain and Ireland.

CHAPTER FIVE

The Solicitor-General stood up respectfully and allowed the Prime Minister to take his chair. Balfour gazed at us silently, each in turn.

'I cannot express my gratitude adequately, gentlemen,' he said slowly. 'I am grateful on behalf of His Majesty's Government that you are willing to undertake the task. Our country is living in perilous times, gentlemen, and this job is vital to our national security.'

The second man still sat in the shadows and was never introduced to us. I have since assumed that the man was some senior staff officer of the Secret Service. At a nod from the Prime Minister, this man rose and placed in our hands some papers, documents binding us to observe some Official Secrets Act which we were asked to read and sign.

'Well, gentlemen,' Balfour smiled thinly after the ceremony was over, 'you are now official agents of His Majesty's Government and I can tell you the facts which lie behind the mission which you are to undertake.'

He cleared his throat in the manner of a lecturer.

'Briefly, our country is facing a grave international

situation. Indeed, I shall go so far as to say that the whole of Europe stands on the brink of an event which could assume catastrophic proportions. The Germans have, for some years, been extending their frontiers and their military capability. You will, perhaps, recall the German Navy Law of 1898 which so effectively increased the size of the German High Seas Fleet?'

The Prime Minister gazed at us keenly.

'Between ourselves, gentlemen, I foresee a war, an inevitable war between ourselves and the Germans. Already German colonial greed is infringing on the borders of our African colonies. Sooner or later there is bound to be a confrontation. The Germans know it and are preparing for it. I, personally, am of the opinion that the war will be fought out in Europe. But that is another matter.'

He paused and collected his thoughts.

'To be precise, the Germans are making preparations for the coming war. At this very moment the German Kaiser Wilhelm is trying to conclude secret treaties with various European countries with the eventual aim of merging them into an alliance against England. He is urging his cousin the Tsar of Russia to form a league with France and Germany against this country.

'As for myself, although England has had her share of conflict with France, I cannot see a French alliance with Germany. The memory of the Franco-Prussian War of 1870 is still too vivid in the Gallic mind. But it is Russia that I am dubious about. The Tsar, I'm afraid, is a weak vacillating gentleman, and unfortunately he rules Russia as an autocrat. What he decides becomes the will of the Russian Empire.'

Raffles coughed politely.

'I have heard that Tsar Nicholas is greatly influenced by his wife, the Tsarina Alexandra Feodorovna, and she, being German, is much disposed towards closer links between the Kaiser and the Tsar on political matters.'

'Just so, Mister Raffles. She has a great influence over the Tsar. Now it happens that His Majesty, King Edward, who is first cousin of Tsar Nicholas, has a very low opinion of his relative. His Majesty is, as you will perhaps know, inclined to be indiscreet at times . . .'

Balfour's voice trailed off. To my mind came recollections of the various scandals associated with the King when he was Prince of Wales. A bevy of actresses and even, so I heard rumour, a kitchen maid were privy to his bedroom on various occasions.

Balfour was speaking again.

'Yes, I'm afraid His Majesty is often indiscreet. He wrote a series of letters to another relative which were . . . well, rather critical of Tsar Nicholas not only in his public life but in his private life. These letters, if they were revealed to the Tsar, would push him into an immediate alliance with his cousin Wilhelm. Just think, gentlemen, of the consequences if the German and Russian Empires combined against England.'

'Is there any reason why these letters should be revealed to the Tsar?' asked Raffles pointedly.

'I'm afraid there is every reason to expect that they will. Last week, on Sunday, May 29, to be precise, the house of a certain relative of His Majesty, to whom these unfortunate letters were sent, was burgled. Among items of jewellery, the letters were also purloined. We now know the theft of the jewellery was a blind and came to suspect a certain German intelligence network which has been operating in this country and which, unfortunately, we have not been able to uncover or destroy.

'One of our agents was able to inform us that the letters have already been delivered to the German Embassy and at this very moment repose in the safe of the assistant military attaché who is an intelligence agent coordinating the spy network.'

'Why don't you arrest the fellow?' I interrupted naïvely.

Balfour gave me a withering glance.

'Embassies and their staffs have diplomatic immunity,' he said heavily. 'Apart from this fact, it is in our interests to allow this man to continue to operate so that we can keep him under observation. It is better the devil you know than the devil you don't. Isn't that so, Carson?'

The Solicitor-General moved his bulky form.

'Quite so, Prime Minister.'

'Who is this military attaché?' queried Raffles.

'What's his name?' grunted Balfour to the Solicitor-General.

'Von Heumann,' replied Carson. 'Oberst Wilhelm von Heumann.'

'Good God!' ejected Raffles, sitting back. 'I've come across that gentleman before. He was a captain then.'

'Yes,' I chimed in excitedly. 'I remember him, too. He was a little German officer, a whipper-snapper with perpendicular moustaches. That was the time when . . .'*

Raffles silenced me with a warning glance.

'It was long ago,' he said shortly. 'So von Heumann is in the German Secret Service?'

'Indeed,' continued the Prime Minister gravely. 'Our source told us that the spy network delivered the letters to von Heumann and they are currently in his safe in the embassy preparatory to being taken out of the country.'

'How can your informant be so certain as to those facts?' demanded Raffles.

The Solicitor-General interrupted.

'Our man worked at the German Embassy.'

'Worked?' queried Raffles.

'We found him in the Thames with a knife in his back six hours ago. He told us this much before he died.'

Balfour sighed sorrowfully.

'A brave man. His father was at Eton with me.'

'And,' said Raffles, 'let me get this quite clear . . . the simple job you have for us is to break into the German Embassy, find von Heumann's safe, open it and steal the letters written by His Majesty?'

'Quite so,' said the Solicitor-General dryly.

* Related in 'The Gift of the Emperor' in *The Amateur Cracksman*, 1899 reprinted with *The Black Mask*, 1901, as *Raffles, The Amateur Cracksman*, 1906.

CHAPTER SIX

Three hours later Raffles and I sat across from each other facing a late supper in the ornate dining rooms of the Reform Club in Pall Mall. It was a club to which I had aspired to gain membership through the influence of my brother-in law, Lord Toby. I was still a little weak and light-headed by the unexpected turn of events. The transition from jailed thief to government agent had been too rapid to allow me to entirely adjust. Raffles, however, sat calmly attacking the cold roast chicken and bottle of chilled Muscadet with a relish I found astonishing.

'I simply can't believe it,' I breathed for perhaps the hundredth time.

Raffles pulled a face.

'It isn't a simple task we have undertaken, Bunny,' he observed, helping himself to the salad. 'In fact it might be better had we opted to serve a term in jail.'

'Why?' I demanded.

'We may be out of our league, old son. Spies, secret agents, are usually rather ruthless individuals who would terminate your existence at the drop of a false moustache.'

I shook my head slowly.

'I'd rather take that risk than the ruin and dishonour! What would Alice have said, returning to find me a convicted felon?'

Raffles was too busy chewing a chicken leg to answer.

A thought made me grin.

'By the Lord Harry, did you see old Mackenzie's face? He was fit to bust! Especially when Carson appointed him our liaison man. I thought he would resign there and then.'

Raffles smiled reflectively.

'It was worth a few days in gaol just to see that,' he agreed.

'What now?' I asked, after the waiter had brought coffee, brandy and cigars.

'After this,' drawled Raffles. 'I shall stroll back to Albany and sleep a good eight hours.'

'No. I meant when do we start our mission.'

'Mission? Lor', Bunny, must you make it sound so melodramatic? My advice to you is to go home, get some sleep and join me for tea tomorrow. Plenty of time to discuss things then. Maybe I shall have worked out some plan. Mackenzie is going to come round at midday with the plans of the embassy and details about the safe.'

I felt vaguely disappointed, as if I was being left out of things.

Raffles leant across the table and patted me on the arm.

'You've had enough excitement during the past few days, Bunny. Take my advice and get some sleep.'

He was right. I did feel terribly tired.

The following afternoon I let myself into his rooms to find him having tea and reading a copy of *The Times*.

'Pour yourself a cup of tea, old chap,' he murmured, reclining in a rather hideous red smoking jacket.

I have always felt a streak of annoyance at Raffles' easy ability to relax in the face of adversity and, for a while, to dismiss pressing problems from his mind. I would have expected, in his place, to be briming with plans for our forthcoming adventure. After all, it is not everyday that one breaks into a foreign embassy to commit a felony on behalf of one's government. Instead, Raffles merely sat back, sipping his tea and viewing the columns of the newspaper with some absorption.

'I see that young bounder Churchill has crossed the floor of the House to join the Liberals,' he remarked while I poured myself some tea.

I was perplexed.

'Churchill? House?'

Raffles gave a deep sigh.

'My dear Bunny, Winston Churchill. He and that other Tory MP, Seeley, have finally resigned from the Party over the Free Trade question. They've been threatening to for months. I never did like the chap. Churchill, I mean. Met him out in South Africa where he was supposed to be a civilian war correspondent but all he did was throw his weight about and try to tell the generals how to conduct the war. Even took part in operations as a combatant, though the generals would have thrown a fit if they had known. No wonder the Boers called him a war criminal and offered a "dead or alive" reward for him. He was a pugnacious ass.'

'I never did go in for politics, Raffles,' I murmured, totally out of my depth.

'Very wise, Bunny,' he replied gravely, but I had a sneaking suspicion there was laughter in those eyes of his.

'Come on, Raffles,' I said in exasperation, 'when are we going to talk about our . . . well, our task?'

Raffles waved a plate of scones under my nose.

'Have one? They're still fairly hot. Another cup of tea?'

I sighed impatiently.

'Don't be in such a hurry, Bunny,' he remonstrated. 'It never does in our line of work. We must take things gently, consider every possibility. This morning I was up at seven o'clock dressed as a window cleaner and plying my trade in Carlton House Terrace outside the German Embassy.'

'You never told me!' I cried indignantly.

'There was no need for two of us on that job,' said Raffles lightly. 'I merely wanted to reconnoitre the place and see if I could spot what type of safe they had.'

'And did you succeed?' I asked eagerly.

'Yes and no,' confessed Raffles. 'I managed to spot the make of the safe but not the type. Actually, I thought they might have indulged in one of their own country's safes, perhaps an Ostertag, but the good Teutons pay our safe makers a compliment by relying on English craftsmen to protect their secrets. They have one of the new Ratner models.'

When it comes to safes and strong rooms Raffles is, as one may already suspect, somewhat of an expert.

'But didn't Mackenzie supply you with details?'

Raffles pulled a face.

'It seems our intelligence men are not all-knowing, after all. They knew the embassy had installed a new safe recently but didn't know what type.'

'Will the safe present a problem?'

Raffles waggled a finger at me.

'All safes present a problem but it is axiomatic that anything man can make, man can break. Unfortunately, I was unable to get a really close look at the safe. I would have liked to see the type or date the model. You can usually tell the date by the serial number.'

'How about cutting our way in?' I said, wishing to air a piece of knowledge picked up from a tale in *The Strand* magazine. Actually, I had purchased the magazine to follow the rather daring confessions of Miss Sarah Bernhardt which *The Strand* was currently serialising but found myself reading a lurid tale by a Mr E. W. Hornung. The villain had cut his way into a steel safe by means of an oxy-acetylene blowtorch.

Raffles' eyes drooped in disapproval.

'My dear Bunny, I trust you know enough about my methods not to associate me with that sort of operation. Besides, modern safes have been created to withstand such attempts. Ever since the blowtorch method was first used, it must have been twenty years ago now in a notorious Birmingham case, if memory serves me right, the safe makers have made their boxes strong enough to resist blowtorches.'

'But,' I cried, trying to justify myself, 'the press say that nothing can withstand a blowtorch attack.'

'*The press!*' sneered Raffles. 'Oxy-acetylene cutting is only satisfactory with ordinary steels but if you take stainless steel, for example, it is powerless. Besides, acetylene is also prohibited for ordinary sale and therefore difficult to get.' He paused. 'I'm told some criminals are using propane or butane as a substitute but,' he waved his hands in dismissal, 'my method is not to load myself up with bulky equipment which takes too much time to set up and is more likely to reduce the contents of the safe to ashes. No, I prefer my own hands and ear on a dial combination and skeleton keys in a good lock.'

'Should we take shooters with us?' I ventured.

Raffles regarded me sorrowfully.

'Shooters? I do believe that you have been reading those penny dreadfuls, old man,' he said sarcastically. 'Shooters, indeed! No, we will not take any firearms. And if you have a pistol in your pocket, Bunny, I suggest you leave it here.'

Reluctantly, I deposited my old service revolver on the table. With an exaggerated air of distaste, Raffles picked it up and laid it in a bureau drawer and locked it.

'Good,' he exclaimed, glancing at the clock. 'Now I think there is time to catch a music hall show before we make our way to the embassy. It will give our minds and bodies a chance to relax. Let's go and see this new show *The Cingalee*. What do you say?'

I always admired Raffles' coolness but the idea of sitting through some musical comedy while waiting for it to get dark enough to break into the German Embassy was a little beyond me. I hesitated. Certainly I realised that seven o'clock on a bright June evening was not the right time to commence our adventure.

'Oh, come on, Bunny,' urged Raffles. 'Don't be such a wet blanket.'

I sighed and nodded but rather unwillingly.

'Jolly good,' he smiled. 'I'll just change into my evening togs, then we can take a cab to your place for you to change.'

I heard him moving about his dressing room, changing for the evening. As he did so, I could hear him singing a chorus of a song made popular by Miss Marie Lloyd from a musical comedy whose name escapes me.

'Every little Jappy chappie's gone upon the Geisha
Trickiest little Geisha ever seen in Asia
I've made things hum a bit, you know, since I became a
  Geisha,
Japanesy, free and easy, tea house girl!'

There were times when I deplored Raffles' taste in popular entertainment.

He eventually emerged from his dressing room in

43

evening kit and carrying some plans which he proceeded to unroll on the table.

'These are the plans of the embassy building which Mackenzie brought around. The idea, old fellow, is to gain entrance from The Mall side of the embassy. We can be easily spotted if we attempt it from the front in Carlton House Terrace. If we hop over this wall into the backyard of the embassy, we could gain entrance through one of these windows. Then all we have to do is make our way down one of these corridors to the front of the building, up these stairs to von Heumann's room which is situated here.'

He stabbed at the plan with the tip of his finger.

'It seems difficult,' I ventured.

Raffles grinned.

'If it was easy do you think our illustrious government would have made such a deal with the likes of you and me?'

'But won't the beastly embassy be filled with Germans?' I persisted.

'Most likely,' he grinned sarcastically. 'It *is* the German embassy.'

'What I mean is, how will we be able to get in and out without being seen? There will be people all over the place.'

'One bridge at a time, Bunny,' admonished Raffles lightly. 'One bridge at a time.'

CHAPTER SEVEN

It was nearly ten-thirty when the theatre audience poured forth into the Strand. I had absolutely no idea what the show, *The Cingalee*, had been about. Unlike Raffles, I was not able to relax and absorb some musical entertainment when every nerve throbbed within me. Again I damned Raffles' easy ability to concentrate his mind and throw off his tension before a job. It was all I could do to stop myself quivering with apprehension. As we came out of the theatre we entered the nether-world of a thick London pea-souper – a world of grey-green rolling fog which narrowed visibility to a few yards. Raffles smiled in satisfaction.

'This suits our purpose most excellently,' he said as he guided me across the Strand towards Charing Cross railway station. There was a large number of people milling around, mainly late night theatre crowds from the suburbs, flocking towards the station and home. I waited by the 'Cross' in front of the station while Raffles went to collect a bag which he had deposited in the Left Luggage department just before the show. It was his small Gladstone bag in which reposed the tools of his profession. He rejoined me in a few moments and turned in the direction of Lyons Corner House. Imagine my surprise when he entered that imposing building with me trailing upon his heels. Late suppers were still being served while a three-piece orchestra manfully scraped out some of the latest popular melodies.

I bit my tongue when Raffles ordered a pot of tea and toast for two and then kept up a steady flow of light conversation, mainly about the musical and the cricket season. After what seemed an age, in reality it was less than an hour later, Raffles drew out his silver Hunter pocketwatch, examined it and summoned a waiter, paid the bill and led the way outside.

If anything, the swirling fog had thickened but Raffles was sure of the way. With an air of nonchalant ease he guided me down to Trafalgar Square, under the Admiralty Arch and into the Mall whose broad thoroughfare made its stately progress towards Buckingham Palace. We soon came abreast of the broad steps which led to Waterloo Place with the tall stone pillar on whose height the Duke of York's statue balanced in its foggy shroud. Raffles paused at these steps and took out his cigarette case, asking me for a light. I could see the way his eyes circled round, trying to penetrate the fog, that this was a ruse on his part and I made a big scene of searching for matches. From the Mall the steps of Waterloo Place led directly into Carlton House Terrace. In spite of the fog we could make out the large house on the right hand side of these steps, facing up into Waterloo Place. This was Lord and Lady Ridley's town house at No 10 Carlton House Terrace. I had chanced to know Lady Ridley back in '98 the year before her marriage, when she was the Honourable Rosamund Guest, the beautiful and sought after daughter of Lord Wimborne. On the opposite side of the steps, to our left, stood No 9 Carlton House Terrace, the imposing edifice of the Imperial German Embassy.

I tried to peer through the odious vapours of the fog and examine its great Regency structure and surrounding high walls.

'It's not going to be easy,' I observed, a sinking feeling in my stomach.

Raffles smiled.

A policeman suddenly emerged from the green shroud and cast a suspicious look in our direction. Raffles clapped me on the shoulder and drew me up the steps, passed the Duke of York's pillar and turned right into Carlton House Terrace in front of the great double oak doors of the embassy. He gave scarce a glance at the building, as if he had no interest in it at all. We continued along the terrace into Carlton House Gardens, passing Lord Curzon's imposing mansion which the Viceroy of India still fully maintained in his absence. I could not help reflecting that India was welcome to him. I had met him once at a soirée given by Lady Ridley and absolutely detested his aristocratic hauteur and pomposity. Another of his ilk, Lord Kitchener, who was now Curzon's commander-in-chief of the army in India, had his town house a short distance away.

Raffles and I slowly walked by these imposing houses and turned left down the small flight of stairs which brought us out, between the houses, back into the Mall.

'It looks impossible,' I whispered, as we traced our steps back to Waterloo Place. 'There is no cover for anyone breaking into the building for this fog cannot be relied upon.'

46

The embassy building was a large one consisting of a basement with separate entrances through small yards and four other floors. Windows gave a view from the building on three sides while the fourth side was bounded by No 8. Between the steps of Waterloo Place and the actual building itself was a small driveway and garden bounded by a high wall. The driveway led to the stables at the back of the building and the stable buildings themselves were actually part of the frontage to the Mall. It seemed obvious that these buildings were occupied by servants. The driveway was effectively sealed off by two tall wrought iron gates. A fencing of wrought iron also stretched across the frontage of the building in which gateways, on either side of the main entrance, led down to the basement area. The main entrance was a porchway flanked by two ornate columns through which some marble steps led up to the oak double doors over which the eagle crest of Imperial Germany rested.

The building seemed virtually impregnable.

'The roof?' I hazarded, peering upwards.

Raffles shook his head.

'Too difficult and too high up. The room we want is on the second floor in the corner that looks out on Waterloo Place and the terrace. Ideally, we want to get in through a ground floor window.'

'Yes, but the basement is constructed so that the yard runs all round the building. Even if we can get over the perimeter wall we would have to climb up to a ground floor window or else get into the basement itself.'

Raffles peered around in the fog and then turned to me.

'Well, Bunny?'

I knew that tone. He *had* a plan and was going to act upon it.

'Ready,' I replied, my heart suddenly beating faster.

He hurried up the steps to a point halfway along the perimeter wall of the embassy building. He paused and gave another swift look around.

'Sharp's the word now, old chap,' he hissed, unlatching his bag and drawing forth a small knotted rope at the end of which was a large metal hook. He flung it towards

47

the top of the wall, which at that point must have been anything between nine and twelve feet in height and which, incidentally, was crowned with a row of metal spikes. The hook caught over the wall and secured the rope. Raffles bent down and extracted what appeared to be a piece of rubber matting rolled up and fastened with string. He latched this over his wrist and was away up the rope as swiftly as he could climb.

My heart nearly stopped. In spite of the swirling fog we were in one of the most exposed parts of the street. It only needed someone to pass down the Mall or come down Waterloo Place to spot us. There was also the hazard that someone might be gazing from one of the many windows of the embassy building or even from the Ridley mansion at No 10 across the other side of the passage.

It seemed an age before Raffles reached the top of the wall, put the rubber mat in place across the spikes, balanced precariously and looked down.

'Come on up, Bunny,' his voice was soft.

Sweating because of fear but obedient, I grasped the knotted rope and heaved myself towards him. As I neared the top I heard rather than saw him swing off the wall and drop beyond. He did this by the simple expediency of gripping two of the spikes and lowering his body to full reach before letting go. He now stood in the shadows of the driveway, an exposed figure from any of the windows of the embassy, and watched me as I balanced on top of the wall.

'Bring the rope up over this side,' he ordered.

I had only just done so when I heard a slow, measured tread coming along the pavement of the passageway we had just quit. The heavy fall of boots was interrupted by a soft whistling. The sounds were familiar to me for there is only one being in London with which they can be associated. A metropolitan policeman! I shinned down the rope for all I was worth and stood pressed against the wall scarce daring to breathe. Raffles had heard the sound too, for he stood very still. The sound of the footsteps passed by towards the front of the embassy and died away.

I gave a deep sigh, shuddering as I realised that had the policeman chanced to peer up at the wall he would have been able to see the rubber mat and the hook which secured our rope. I shinned up a couple of feet and took down the rubber mat. Then I hung on to one of the spikes while unhooking the rope and finally slipped back down the wall.

'Well done, Bunny,' whispered Raffles, replacing the mat and the rope in his bag. Then he grinned. 'Step one completed.'

I was quaking in my boots for we were still exposed to any person who happened to glance through the windows. Raffles led the way across the drive to the side of the building and surveyed the situation rapidly. A small yard, maybe four feet wide, ran like a moat around the basement floor. It was going to be impossible to break in through a ground floor window.

'The basement it will have to be,' muttered Raffles.

Without more ado he lowered himself the eight feet or so into the yard, with me following closely. I noticed that Raffles took extra care not to make any superfluous noise. He later told me that the Germans had a particular fondness for keeping a rather savage breed of guard dogs called Alsatians which could maim a man quite easily. If such dogs were loose in the grounds we did not see any of them. I was certainly thankful Raffles made no mention of them at the time.

He checked several of the side windows carefully before choosing one which he thought suitable for his purpose. Then he set down his bag and, with the aid of a hooded flashlight, produced what appeared to be a piece of putty wrapped in a damp cloth. He pressed this against the window pane near the window-latch and inserted a small piece of wood in it. Then, from his pocket, he drew out what I thought was a clasp knife. With this he scratched at the window and then tugged at the wood which came away with the putty attached to a small rectangle of glass. This he deposited in his bag.

I saw him grin as he reached his hand inside the hole and a second later the window was swinging open.

It was a matter of seconds before we had climbed over the sill.

'And now,' hissed Raffles, 'we come to the difficult part.'

With the aid of his flashlight, we crossed through what was apparently a large pantry. It was full of pots and pans, kitchen utensils and stacks of tableware and cutlery. From a small door we emerged into a darkened corridor. I was thankful that Raffles had memorised the plans of the building that Mackenzie had supplied him with. I followed him blindly. The corridor ended in a sort of servants' hall, thankfully deserted. A circular iron stairway spiralled up to the ground floor and Raffles had no hesitation in making the ascent. Now we stood in a dimly lit corridor which was carpeted with a luxurious deep pile that muffled our footsteps completely.

Without hesitation, Raffles led the way along this corridor which opened into a central hall. It was rather like a palace with marble stairways, high painted ceilings and sombre looking statues. A polished wooden table stood in the centre on which were placed a number of German magazines. A life size portrait of Kaiser Wilhelm II gazed disapprovingly down on us from above an ornate marble fireplace while smaller portraits scowled or smiled from the other walls. They all appeared to be scions of the house of Hohenzollern. Looking singularly out of place among them, the late Graf von Bismarck grimaced in annoyance from the foot of the stairway.

Raffles was about to step out into the hall when a sharp voice echoed down the stairs.

'*Wie spät ist es? Meine Uhr geht nach!*'

Raffles stepped hastily back, treading on my foot so that I had to stifle my groan of agony. We pressed back against the wall of the corridor as, from a door on the far side of the hall, a man in shirt sleeves and obviously a porter came out and peered up the stairwell.

'*Mitternach, Herr Oberst.*'

'*Ist eine Nachricht für mich da?*'

'*Nein, Herr Oberst.*'

'*Danke, das ist alles.*'

The man in shirt sleeves shrugged and turned back into his room.

Raffles paused for a moment and then stepped into the hall, looking swiftly up the stair. Whoever had stood there a moment before had disappeared. Treading carefully, with me only a step behind, he went swiftly through the hall and up the stairs. No one was about. He passed down another corridor and came to a door which bore the legend: 'Oberst von Heumann'. Cautiously he reached out and tried the handle. The door was locked. It was but the work of a few moments for Raffles to take out his ring of skeleton keys and find one to suit his purpose. We passed into a darkened office and Raffles re-locked the door behind us.

I leant against a desk breathing rather heavily, feeling the nervous tension causing all manner of spasms within my stomach.

Raffles made no comment but made a detailed survey of the room with his flashlight. Its beam came to rest on a grim-faced portrait of a German admiral. I recognised the threatening features of Von Tirpitz, one of the new German war lords who had recently been instrumental in getting the Reichstag, the German parliament, to approve his plan to double the strength of the German navy.

'That's our meat,' hissed Raffles moving across the room to the portrait. He put down his bag and lifted the picture from its hook. Sure enough, behind the portrait, set in the wall of the room, was the door to a safe.

Raffles turned and grinned.

'There you are, Bunny. What did I tell you? That's a Ratner.'

I grimaced and took my stand near the study door. We had made an arrangement that I was to leave him to 'crack' the safe while I kept guard.

One ear against the study door, I saw Raffles bending towards the safe, one hand holding the flashlight steady on the dial and the other twirling the tumblers. Ten minutes passed and still nothing had happened. Raffles paused in his endeavours and I could see him wiping the sweat from his face and hands with a large handkerchief. I went across to join him. He was grim-faced in the semi-gloom.

'Damn it, Bunny!' he swore softly. 'I knew that I should have done a little more homework on Ratner's new lines. I swear that Daniel Ratcliffe has surpassed himself with this design. I just can't seem to get the tumblers in the right sequence.'

I shook my head in dumb astonishment. It is very rare that Raffles confessed to a lack of ability when it came to opening a safe.

He returned to his task and motioned me to resume my stand by the door.

I had been in position hardly a moment when I thought I heard a sound in the corridor.

'*Cave!*' I hissed and Raffles froze, his eyes in my direction.

I pressed my ear against the door.

Yes, I could hear the sound of voices. The stentorian tone of the man whom the porter had addressed as 'Herr Oberst' and the higher pitch of a woman's voice came through the wooden partition. The voices grew louder and paused outside the door. I stood numb with terror. The handle was rattled. I thanked God that Raffles had locked the door behind us. The man was saying something. Apologising. He said something about '*meinen Schlüssel*' and then his voice receded. By a miracle he seemed to have forgotten his key.

'Quick!' I whispered, 'they are coming in!'

In a trice he had the portrait back in place and his quickly darting eyes had spotted the only hiding place in the room – behind the tall baize curtains which were drawn across the wall length windows. Raffles had barely time to seize his bag and crowd with me behind the curtains before there came a rattling at the door and it was pushed open.

CHAPTER EIGHT

The lights were switched on almost before we had time to adjust the curtains. Raffles had taken up his stance so that he could peer out into the room through the central gap while I was pushed into a corner with no view at all. I was about to resign myself to this frustrating position when I spied a tiny hole and silently gave praise to the diligent work of moths among the baize drapes. I now craned my neck forward and applied my eye to the tiny hole.

The first thing I saw was a very familiar face.

It had been many years since Raffles and I went on our ill-fated cruise on the *Uhlan* of the Norddeutscher Lloyd Line but I would have recognised von Heumann anywhere. There he stood on the threshold in the dress uniform of a colonel of hussars, a little older, true, but still the same man. He stood fingering his moustaches, curling them into twin spires and staring through his rimless glasses. There was the same murderous scar across one of his cheeks which had been a present from his student duelling days at Heidelberg. He had paused for a moment and then stood aside.

'Come in, Baroness, come in,' he said, giving a slight bow from the waist.

The woman that entered was, without doubt, one of the most beautiful that I have ever beheld. I mean no disloyalty to Alice when I say it but I think even she would agree that this Baroness was one of those women who, upon entering a room, would still the conversation and turn the heads of all present. She was tall, with dark reddish hair. It was difficult to tell whether it was auburn or a strange mixture of dark brown and red. She carried her well-proportioned figure as if used to commanding and being obeyed. Even from the uncomfortable position of my spy-hole I could see her skin was pale, almost creamy, with a delicate blush of red against her cheeks. Her eyes flashed darkly in the artificial light.

'Herr Fuchs is not here?'

The voice was a tremulous soprano.

'No, Baroness. He is a little late. Will you be seated?'

The beautiful vision sank into a chair which, annoyingly, was just beyond my range of vision. Almost immediately there came a tap upon the door.

'Come!' commanded von Heumann.

Someone entered; a little man in a greatcoat and muffler.

'Ah, Moltke,' said von Heumann to the newcomer. 'Is Herr Fuchs with you?'

'No. He is not here then?'

I strained to follow the German, wishing I had paid more attention to that confounded language whilst at school.

There was a silence.

'I hear that the Englander was found?' It was the voice of the man called Moltke.

I found it annoying that all three were beyond the range of my vision.

'Yes,' von Heumann returned. 'They fished him out of the Thames the other day. The police have been here asking questions.'

'It was not a wise thing to do,' came the voice of the Baroness. 'The deed could easily be trace back to the embassy.'

'Baroness von Stalhein,' it was von Heumann again, 'there was no choice. The man was an English agent. Somehow or another he managed to obtain a job here, at the embassy, by pretending to be a Bavarian. He was discovered opening the safe in this very room. Whether he knew the letters were contained there or not we were unable to discover . . . he did not speak much. However, all things considered, we had no other course open to us but elimination. On no account could we let him report back to his superiors.'

'Providing he had not done that already, von Heumann.'

There was a new voice in the room, a sharp, brittle voice, whose tone was oddly familiar to me. I could not

54

place it. I peered through my spy-hole but the man who had entered had already passed from view and all I could see was one shoulder of the shadowy figure standing with his back to the curtain.

'Herr Fuchs,' von Heumann's voice sounded nervous. 'We were waiting for you.'

'It is not always easy to pass in and out of the embassy without prying eyes watching every movement,' replied the newcomer.

'Perhaps it was not a good idea to meet here like this,' came the low voice of the Baroness.

'It was orders. Von Heumann's handling of the English agent has led to an embarrassing situation,' replied the man addressed as Herr Fuchs.

There was a shuffling sound and I could mentally see von Heumann uncomfortably shifting his weight.

'For God's sake, von Heumann, if the Englander was to be killed why didn't you simply hide his body so that their Secret Service would be left guessing? Or why didn't you at least make an attempt to let the killing appear accidental? Instead you let his body be found in the Thames – so messy and clumsy.'

'But, Herr Fuchs, it was the only thing to do at the time,' came von Heumann's aggrieved tone.

'I have already had a private interview with the ambassador. He is very irate that the integrity of his position has suffered by this misfortune. A full report on the matter is being sent to Berlin.'

'We cannot spend our time on simple recriminations, Herr Fuchs,' came Baroness von Stalhein's voice. 'We all know that von Heumann's action was in error. An inquest will not alter the situation.'

'You are quite correct, Baroness,' returned the voice of Herr Fuchs. 'The situation is this: – the English Secret Service know one of their agents is dead. I feel we must assume that they know we have their king's letters. The exact extent of their knowledge remains in doubt. Can we be sure that their agent did not inform his superiors of the whereabouts of the letters before he . . . er, died?'

'He had no time to do so, Herr Fuchs. I saw to that,'

protested von Heumann.

'The way you see to things seems a trifle inefficient, Herr Oberst,' replied Herr Fuchs evenly. 'I think that we must assume that the English know we have the letters and where they are. They may even be planning an attempt on the safe.'

'Robbing the embassy?' von Heumann's voice was astounded. 'Impossible!'

I felt myself go cold. Any moment now I felt that the steel-like voice of Herr Fuchs would denounce our hiding place.

'The English are not fools. I think Herr Fuchs is right.' It was the Baroness again.

'Quite so. We must therefore transfer the letters to another place of safety. Open the safe von Heumann.'

'Another place of safety?' It was Moltke who spoke.

'Would it not be best to send them directly to Berlin now?' asked von Heumann.

Herr Fuchs chuckled. It was a cold sort of chuckle, without warmth or humour.

'Certainly. Do we post them? Is that what you have in mind?'

'Of course not. I meant that we could send them in the diplomatic bag,' came von Heumann's surly tone.

Herr Fuchs' voice was like ice.

'Since you have drawn attention to this embassy, von Heumann, and since we must assume that the English know we have the letters, do you think their Secret Service will respect the privileges of the diplomatic bag? My dear, Oberst!'

'What is to be done?' asked Moltke, breaking the uncomfortable silence which followed.

'I will take the letters with me and deposit them in a safe place until next week. Then I shall personally hand them over to the special courier who will take them to Berlin.'

There was a metallic clang as von Heumann opened the safe.

'Here is the package Herr Fuchs.'

There was a silence during which I imagined Herr

Fuchs checked the contents of the package.

'Good. All is in order.'

Someone coughed. It was Moltke.

'There is the matter of *Der Erpresser* to be sorted out, Herr Fuchs.'

I frowned, not understanding the word from my scant vocabulary.

'Ah yes. A very stupid man, Moltke. He is to be eliminated forthwith.'

'Another death?' There was a tone of rebuke in von Heumann's voice.

'Yes,' came the cold reply. 'But unlike your fiasco, Herr Oberst, our friend is to meet with an accident, an accident no one will question. One more tragic death among the flotsam and jetsam of the poverty-stricken area in which he lives will not be questioned. Is that understood, Moltke?'

'Perfectly, Herr Fuchs.'

'That is good. Now, I am going home to my bed.'

'But what of us?' It was the Baroness.

'After next week we shall disband and go our separate ways. We have achieved two years of effort in this country without detection and the obtaining of these letters is a suitable climax to our activities. It would be tempting fate to continue our activities.'

'But, Herr Fuchs, the weekend is still arranged, is it not?' asked the Baroness.

'The party? Yes, we shall all be there. It will be a unique opportunity to pump the old British sea-dog for information. But that will be the last time we gather together. Understood?'

I had a brief glimpse of a shadowy figure pass from the room and cursed that I was unable to pick out any recognisable features. I knew that it would become imperative to identify the mysterious Herr Fuchs who was apparently the chief of the spy network which had stolen the letters. The man Moltke followed with a grunt of farewell. Then the Baroness von Stalhein bade von Heumann a cold 'goodnight' and also left.

There was a bang as von Heumann closed the safe and

sounds as if he were seating himself at his desk. There came to my ears the sound of a bottle being opened and a drink poured into a glass, followed by an uncouth smacking of lips. I recalled von Heumann had been fond of Westphalian Steinhager Schnapps and wondered whether he was feeding that fondness.

God knows how long it was that Raffles and I had to stand rooted to the spot. It was certainly more than an hour. I was nearly crying with cramp when von Heumann finally rose from his desk, walked to the door, snapped off the lights and locked the door behind him.

'Are you all right, Bunny?' whispered Raffles.

'Stiff as a poker,' I groaned, gently prodding my legs and feeling the pins and needles tingling through them. It took a while to get the circulation going properly again.

Raffles was looking rueful.

'Beaten by a short head,' he remarked, staring wistfully at the safe.

'Not our fault, old boy,' I replied, trying to massage my knee.

'If only we could track down this man Fuchs. Still, we do have a few days. It's only Wednesday now and Fuchs said it would be next week before the letters were passed over.'

'Wouldn't it be better to get out of here before ruminating about that?' I ventured.

'Come on then, old chap,' grinned Raffles.

Our exit from the embassy building turned out to be even easier than our ingress. Within ten minutes we were strolling calmly up Waterloo Place, passing the frowning bust of General John Fox Burgoyne. We hurried across Pall Mall and turned into St James's Square where a portly constable saluted us and bade us a cheerful 'good morning'. There was a pinkish hint of dawn in the sky as we made our way via York Street, pass St James' Church and across the deserted thoroughfare of Piccadilly to Albany.

Once in his rooms Raffles set about preparing hot coffee.

'We simply have to track down this bounder Fuchs,' he

said, as he poured the coffee.

'I don't see how,' I replied. 'And, after all, we've done what the Prime Minister wanted us to do.'

'But not accomplished it,' pointed out Raffles.

'But the conditions were not dependent on our being successful,' I argued.

Raffles shot me a shrewd look.

'You're not worried about the dangers, are you Bunny?'

I flushed.

'Well, they do sound a tough bunch to come up against,' I admitted. 'Why,' memory flooded my mind, 'they are even planning to kill someone else . . . er someone called *Der Erpresser*. What's that mean?'

'The blackmailer,' replied Raffles and became suddenly thoughtful. 'I wonder what that is all about? You know, if we knew who the blackmailer was he might be someone who could give us information about the group.'

'If we were able to track him down before Moltke,' I observed.

There came a sharp knock on the door. I frowned as Raffles went to the door and returned with the dour face of Mackenzie looming behind.

'Mon, 'tis our auld acquaintence Mackenzie o' Scoteland Yaard an' Scoteland itsel',' he grinned.

'Enough of the wise cracks, Mister Raffles,' grunted Mackenzie. 'D'ye have the letters? Have ye been successful?'

'My dear Detective Chief Superintendent,' smiled Raffles indulgently, 'just bear with us a moment while we have some coffee and toast and then you may escort us to Sir Edward where all shall be revealed. I presume you have some means of conveyance outside?'

Mackenzie gave a surly nod.

He fretted with ill-concealed impatience while we gulped down our coffee and swallowed our toast.

Within half an hour the carriage had halted in King Charles Street and we were conducted through a side door into the Home Office. In a very rapid and breathless fashion we were led down a maze of corridors and entered a well lit sitting room where, astonishingly, Sir Edward Carson rose to meet us fully dressed and looking as fresh and confident as if it were a normal time of day.

'Have you been successful?' were his first words.

His face fell when Raffles shook his head.

Carson had remarkable self-control and motioned us to be seated. Mackenzie, however, remained standing near the door, twisting his bowler hat nervously in his hands. Carson sat without speaking as Raffles briefly told of our adventures. When he had finished, Carson leant back in his chair, pressing the tips of his fingers together and closing his eyes. His mouth quirked in disappointment.

'So the letters are already on their way to Berlin?' he asked in a low voice.

'They will not be handed to the courier before next week,' replied Raffles. 'You know how the Germans like keeping to timetables. In the meantime they are in Fuchs' possession.'

Carson sighed deeply.

'But we know nothing of this man, whoever he is.'

'Begging your pardon, sir,' Mackenzie interrupted brightly, 'but Scotland Yard could easily track down a foreigner residing in London under the name of Fuchs.'

Carson looked at Mackenzie rather pityingly, so I thought.

'On the contrary, Chief Superintendent, apart from the fact that the name Fuchs is a very common German name, it also means "the Fox" from which I deduce that it is the code name for the head of this group and not his real name.'

Mackenzie's face fell and he blushed in embarrassment as Carson turned his gaze back to Raffles.

'We have no idea of where or when Fuchs will transfer the letters to the courier? We have no idea who the courier will be?' As Raffles shrugged, Carson bit his lip. 'If only you had been an hour or so earlier . . .'

'It is no good reflecting on what might have been,' said Raffles, admonishing the Solicitor-General. 'However, we could try to track down Fuchs through one of the others. Does the intelligence service have any details about the other people we saw?'

Carson shuffled through some papers on his desk.

'We already know von Heumann is an assistant military attaché and a rather fumbling intelligence officer. As for Baroness von Stalhein, she has been staying in this country for the past year as a guest of Countess von Wolff-Mitternich, the ambassador's wife. She is staying at the ambassadorial residence with her younger brother Erich who is some kind of aide to the ambassador. Moltke is employed as a minor clerk at the embassy while Fuchs is an entire mystery. Finding him would be like searching for a needle in a haystack.'

'Nevertheless,' said Raffles, 'one of his group must know a means of establishing contact with him.'

Carson raised an eyebrow and looked at Raffles keenly.

'You mean to pursue the matter, Mister Raffles? You have some plan?'

'Yes. Give Bunny and me the authority to track down members of this group and see if we can find a way of getting to Fuchs.'

'You would only have a few days,' observed Carson.

'We've been up against stiffer odds before,' vowed Raffles.

'You make it sound a possibility,' mused Carson.

'Och,' interrupted Mackenzie. 'I canna say that I'd recommend it, sir. We don't even know for sure whether yon pair even attempted the safe. I wouldna trust them.'

Raffles swung round on the policeman with a bitter smile.

'I must say that is rather churlish of you, Mackenzie. But perhaps I should expect no less.'

It was Carson who admonished the Chief Superintendent.

'You will remember that Mister Raffles and Mister Manders are now agents working on behalf of His Majesty's Government. No matter their past, their word is that of gentlemen.'

Mackenzie turned red and muttered something inaudible.

'You already hold authority to act in this matter,' went

on Carson to Raffles. 'If you can find a way of tracing Fuchs and getting hold of the letters, the country will be greatly indebted to you. Unless you have an objection, Mackenzie here will continue to act as your liaison with us. If you require anything, material assistance, information or finance, Mackenzie will be placed under instruction to provide it. Is that understood, Mackenzie?'

Mackenzie glowered under his bushy eyebrows.

'Aye, sir,' he muttered.

'All we require at this stage,' smiled Raffles, 'is the addresses of where von Heumann, the Baroness and the man Moltke are staying. The baroness, you say, lives at the ambassador's residence?'

The Solicitor-General nodded.

'As guest of the ambassador. Von Heumann has rooms in a private hotel in Pall Mall while Moltke has some sort of apartment in Pimlico. Here are the addresses.'

Raffles took the paper and thanked Carson.

The Solicitor-General stood up and shook us both warmly by the hand.

'I wish you luck, gentlemen. Remember it is imperative that those letters are not allowed to become a political tool in the Kaiser's hands.'

'We will do our best, sir,' Raffles assured him as we both turned to go.

CHAPTER NINE

'We'll have to buck up, Bunny,' Raffles said. He had just shaken me awake from a deep sleep and I was yawning fretfully on his chaise-longue whilst he poured me a cup of tea.

'What's the time?'

'Nearly two o'clock in the afternoon,' replied Raffles, thrusting the cup at me and munching some toast. 'We want to take a look round Moltke's rooms before he returns from the embassy.'

'What's the plan?'

'I haven't really worked one out, old chap. That is, apart from going to Moltke's rooms and searching to see if we can find anything that will lead us to Fuchs.'

I reached out for the hot buttered toast.

'And if there isn't?'

Raffles gave a half shrug as if he had not contemplated the idea.

'Wouldn't it be better if Mackenzie arrested Moltke and forced the information out of him?'

Raffles shook his head sorrowfully at me.

'My dear Bunny, the man is a professional spy. They're a breed apart. According to the popular magazines they all take poison rather than confess.'

We said little while we finished our breakfast, spruced up and issued forth from Albany in search of a Hansom to take us to Pimlico. Raffles dismissed the cab at the intersection of Lupus Street and Denbigh Street, two wide thoroughfares with Denbigh Street pushing northward to the splendid edifice of Victoria Railway Station. Moreton Place, where Moltke had his rooms, was a small stretch of street at the back of the main road. It was a border region in which people with pretensions could opt for living in Belgravia rather than Pimlico. We walked along, passed numerous tenement houses, and came to a bleak looking place whose front steps were guarded by a large, grim faced woman. She stood with folded muscular arms and coarse black hair drawn back into a bun. She surveyed passers-by with a scowl of contempt. Her expression did not alter as Raffles and I approached her.

'Good afternoon, madam,' Raffles opened, raising his hat.

The woman grunted. It might have been a friendly response but it sounded more like a threatening growl.

Raffles replaced his hat, still forcing a smile.

'Is this the residence of Mister Moltke?'

The woman's eyes narrowed and assumed a hard glint.

'Police?'

The word was a staccato bark which made me jump nervously.

'Friends,' countered Raffles with one of his disarming smiles.

His hand went out at which the woman responded and something slipped between them; something which altered her attitude a little.

She smiled. It was rather a grotesque smile.

'You means 'im wot's a foreign gennelman?'

'The same,' affirmed Raffles.

'*H*upstairs. Second floor front.'

She turned sideways so that Raffles and I could move past her bulky form. The dingy corridor of the old house had a peculiar odour of camphor. It reminded me of a visit to a funeral parlour where I had once been forced after the untimely decease of a relative. We went up the darkened stairway to the second floor where Raffles paused before a sturdy door and knocked.

Almost immediately a door further along the landing opened.

'You wantin' the 'Un?'

It was a ferret-faced man whose reddy eyes and pointed features and weedy appearance seemed to be a caricature of a human being.

'Hun? The German? Yes,' nodded Raffles.

''Un's awt!' spat the man in disgust. 'Polis!'

The door slammed.

Raffles grinned at me.

'Doesn't seem that the occupants of this place have much respect for the constabulary, eh Bunny?'

He dragged forth his bunch of skeleton keys, examined the lock and selected one. I never cease to marvel at Raffles' professionalism and ability. The key turned in the lock at the first attempt.

We stepped into a room whose odours were even more pungent than those of the corridor. The smell of alcohol and stale smoke were almost overpowering. Several empty bottles lay discarded; their labels proclaiming their contents to have been distilled by Mister William

Teacher of Glasgow. There were several unemptied ashtrays. The curtains had not been drawn back and the bed was unmade. The aspect was one of complete disorder.

Raffles shut the door carefully behind us and surveyed the room with an expression of utter distaste. Then he crossed to the window and drew back one of the curtains to let a little more light fall upon the scene.

'Well, Bunny, I suppose we'd better set to. You start over there and I'll start here.'

'What are we looking for?' I ventured.

'Scraps of paper, letters, anything which might give a clue as to where and who this man Fuchs is.'

We must have spent upwards of an hour ferreting through the room without learning much about the man Moltke. That he drank too much, smoked too much and was slovenly in his personal habits we could easily deduce. He also had a prediliction to rather vulgar literature, judging by the numerous 'penny dreadfuls' that lay scattered round the room.

I was about to tell Raffles that I considered we were wasting our time, for there was absolutely no sign of any personal papers, when there came an abrupt rattle at the door. Before we could move, it swung open and a man stood on the threshold regarding us in astonishment. He was a small man, well muffled in spite of the warm June weather. I had no difficulty in recognising the figure of Moltke from the previous evening. His jaw dropped but he had quick reflexes, I'll give the man that. His hand snaked to his pocket and reappeared bearing a wicked looking Luger pistol of the type that were frequently used by the Boers during the war.

'You will be so good as to raise your hands,' his voice was soft but held a cold edge to it. 'Now!'

We did so.

Moltke stepped inside the room and closed the door behind him.

I felt a shiver of apprehension. The man was a killer; he would shoot without compunction.

'Who are you?'

65

The barrel of his pistol described a circle between Raffles and I.

'Speak, before I call the police!'

Raffles smiled.

'Ah . . . the police. By all means call them.'

Moltke's eyes narrowed.

'So?' The word was an expression of understanding. 'Who are you? Secret Service? Scotland Yard?'

'Moltke,' Raffles' voice held a bantering quality. I was astounded at his coolness. 'Moltke, the game – as they say – is up. We are prepared to strike a bargain with you.'

'*Donnerwetter*!' Moltke's voice was a harsh bark. '*You* bargain? Perhaps you have not noticed that this is a pistol in my hand. I can assure you that it is loaded and you will notice that I have caught you in the act of breaking into my rooms. There is a law against this action. I can shoot you both out of hand.'

For a moment I thought he was going to suit the action to the word. Perspiration started to gather on my forehead.

'Come now, Moltke, surely you do not think we are stupid?' Raffles' voice was on a sharper key. 'We know all about Fuchs' network.'

Only by a blink of his eyes did Moltke reveal his surprise. He had most amazing self-control.

'Yes,' went on Raffles, 'we know all about you, von Heumann, the Baroness and Fuchs. The game is up.'

Moltke frowned and bit his lip.

'What is this bargain which you offer?' he asked suspiciously.

'Quite simple. We'll turn a blind eye to you leaving the country if you can tell us where we can pick up Fuchs.'

'*Dummkopf*!' Moltke suddenly laughed. 'You think to fool me. You know a lot, yes, but I do not betray my leader!'

'Bunny!' Raffles cry made me start.

Moltke's eyes flickered towards me, thinking that Raffles was issuing an instruction for me to act. The Luger swung up. God, but how cunning Raffles can be. In that split second, he reached down and seized an overfilled ashtray, hurling its contents into the face of Moltke. The man staggered back a pace clawing at his eyes and coughing as the cigarette ash filled his mouth.

I don't know how I did it but I found my limbs galvanised into action. Moltke had been standing on a rug. I bent down and jerked it hard so that he lost his balance and his pistol went flying across the room. Raffles and he made a grab for it at the same time but Raffles was there first. He seized the gun by the barrel and, in one swift motion, struck Moltke across the face. He went down grunting in pain.

'There now, old chap,' Raffles sighed. 'That's better.' He grinned at me. 'A smart bit of work that, Bunny. Well done.'

I was still quivering with nerves.

'Now, Moltke, where were we? I think you were about to say something about the whereabouts of Fuchs.'

Moltke glowered.

We had all risen cautiously to our feet.

'What's the matter, Moltke?' asked Raffles after a moment's silence. 'Cat got your tongue?'

Moltke frowned.

'Please?'

'We are waiting to hear what you have to say,' I explained.

'I say nothing,' returned Moltke sulkily. 'You may do what you like.'

'In that case, sit down Moltke,' Raffles waved to a chair near the window. Then, as if in afterthought: 'Bunny, let a little air in here like a good chap.'

Frowning, I opened the window and stepped back.

Raffles was gazing thoughtfully at Moltke and then, to my surprise, he stood up and pocketed the gun.

'I'm going to go downstairs and telephone Mackenzie. Just watch over our prisoner. I shan't be long.'

I swallowed nervously.

'I say, Raffles, I can send the message to Mackenzie.'

Raffles looked at me with a suggestion of a sneer.

'Not nervous, are you?'

Oh, how I hated him then.

'I should say not!' I retorted indignantly. How could he show me up in front of Moltke?

'Good. Shan't be a jiffy.'

He turned to go.

'I say!' I called desperately, crossing the room after him. 'How about leaving me the pistol?'

Raffles' mouth quirked.

'Now we don't want any accidents, do we Bunny? I'll take the gun. Don't worry, the fight has been knocked out of him and I shan't be a moment.'

I had no chance to protest further.

I turned back into the room and took up a stand with folded arms leaning against the door jamb. Moltke was regarding me with a curious smile.

'You are nervous, Englishman,' he said softly. 'You are not like your companion.'

My face reddened.

'Utter bosh! Don't try anything with me or you'll damn well see what I'm made of!' I snarled back.

He sneered.

Then, before I could bat an eyelid, he had sprung from his chair, leapt for the window and was through it.

With a cry of astonishment I was after him. At first I thought the man had committed suicide. After all, we were on the second floor. What I had not realised when I opened the window, and what Raffles too had apparently not realised, was that a fire escape ran down the side of the window to a first floor balcony. Moltke was already on the balcony.

'Halt!' I cried, swinging my leg over the sill.

A hand fell on my shoulder.

I paused, startled. It was Raffles.

'Don't be so fast, Bunny,' he said smilingly. 'Give him more of a head start.'

My jaw dropped.

'What do you mean?'

'My plan is going like clockwork,' he said blandly. 'Moltke is going to lead us to Fuchs. All we have to do is follow.'

I stared at Raffles aghast.

'You mean it was planned? You mean you purposely left the room knowing that Moltke was going to make a bolt for it. You banked that I would be incompetent enough to let him? What if he had another gun? I might have been killed!'

I cursed his damnable aplomb.

'But you are not, are you?' he returned calmly. 'Stop grousing, Bunny. I apologise if I've upset you. Now let's get after the bounder.'

Raffles pushed me aside and started down the fire escape. I was speechless with rage and had it not been for a sense of higher duty I would have let him go alone. However, on reflection, I had made a bargain with the Solicitor-General just as Raffles had. So I cursed him silently and followed.

Moltke had run along the balcony across the frontage of three houses and was now starting down some fire escape steps to the street.

'We mustn't lose him!' cried Raffles as we clambered after him. 'On the other hand we musn't follow too closely. After a while, he must think we have been shaken off and that he has lost us. That'll give him a chance to make a bee-line for Fuchs.'

'What makes you think he'll go to Fuchs?' I gasped.

'Because he knows we know something about the network but that we don't know who Fuchs is. He will try to warn Fuchs and then disperse the network.'

By the time we reached the street Moltke's form was disappearing into Denbigh Street. We ran swiftly along, scattering irate pedestrians who cursed us heartily. Several small children ran with us cheering wildly until we outdistanced them. At Denbigh Street we looked up and down the straight thoroughfare and my heart fell when we could see no sign of our quarry. Then Raffles gave an exclamation and pointed. There was our man running down Charlwood Street and I thanked God for the architect who had designed the long wide streets of this area.

We spent an hour keeping track of Moltke as he sped from one street to another eventually emerging onto the Buckingham Palace Road. Here he hailed a cab but, thankfully, a second cab plying for hire was coming along and we signalled it to stop, breathlessly climbing in. Raffles ordered the driver to follow Moltke's cab but not too closely.

The driver grimaced bitterly.

'Polis, eh? 'Spose I'll have to wait months for my fare until Scotland Yard make out your chits. Just my luck.'

Silently Raffles handed the man a half-sovereign.

'Cor! You're a toff, mister!' The man ceased his grumbling immediately. 'Don't you fear, I'll not lose him.'

We followed Moltke's Hansom down Buckingham Palace Road into Eaton Terrace and then down Cliveden Place into Sloane Square. The Hansom circled the square three times and then set off at a brisk pace down King's Road. Just past the big military barracks, the head-quarters of the Duke of York's Regiment, Moltke's cab made a sudden turn down Cheltenham Terrace and then into Franklin's Row and then another rapid turn into Royal Hospital Road. Our driver, as good as his word, kept pace with these rapid manoeuvres but did not follow too closely. Moltke's cab turned into Chelsea Bridge Road and suddenly stopped at the entrance of Ranelagh Gardens. The German climbed out and paid off the cab, standing looking up and down the street before disappearing into the gardens.

Our cabby had halted some way away and Raffles and I climbed out. Raffles paid the man and tipped him at which the cabby assured him, once again, that he was a toff an' no mistake! We walked rapidly to the main entrance of Ranelagh Gardens, through which Moltke had disappeared, and entered one of the most lovely parks with which London is endowed. There were few people about in spite of the late afternoon sunshine. We strolled along a path keeping wary eyes open for our man.

Suddenly Raffles gripped me by the arm and pointed.

'There he is, Bunny. Sitting on that park bench.'

Sure enough, Moltke was seated on a bench, his back towards us facing towards another entrance to the gardens.

'Looks like he is waiting for someone,' said Raffles excitedly. 'Perhaps he is waiting for Fuchs. We'll take our stand by that clump of trees,' he nodded to a cluster of yew trees a short distance away. 'It's my guess that Moltke thinks he has thrown us off the scent and this is a rendezvous spot for the group.'

Raffles' excitement was infectious and momentarily I forgave him for playing me such a churlish trick as he had in the Moreton Place tenement. It might not have been cricket but at least Raffles' plan had brought results.

We stood behind the trees with a good view of Moltke and waited. The time passed and Moltke simply sat there. First a half hour went by, then an hour and then an hour-and-a-half. It was growing deuced uncomfortable. It was nearly two hours and Moltke had not even shifted his position on the seat. His contact was obviously late but he sat there patiently. More patiently than I could have sat in the circumstances.

'Ah h'mm . . .' A uniformed park attendant approached us with a suspicious look on his face. I supposed that it must have looked damnably funny, the sight of two men lurking behind a clump of trees for two hours. 'Excuse me, gentlemen, I'm afraid the gardens are closing in ten minutes. If you don't mind leaving now . . .?' He shot us another suspicious look and passed on.

Raffles sighed deeply.

'I'm afraid the plan hasn't worked, Bunny,' he said regretfully. 'Moltke must know he has not lost us. He must know that we are here.'

'You mean he's been fooling us all this time? He's just been sitting there doing nothing, knowing that we were watching him?'

'I'm afraid so. Well, let's go and pick him up. Maybe you are right, after all. Perhaps Mackenzie will be able to get some information out of him.'

There was no mistaking the disappointment on Raffles' face.

We walked up to Moltke. He didn't move as we came up.

'All right, Moltke,' said Raffles as we approached. 'You've won for the time being. Now you'll have to take your chances with the authorities.'

Still Moltke made no movement.

We walked round to the front of the bench. It was then I noticed that Moltke's head was slumped on his chest, his hands lying loosely at his sides. There was a small brown bottle near one of them.

Raffles suppressed an exclamation.

He bent forward and lifted Moltke's head up by the chin.

The face was pale, the eyes shut and the lips curiously blue.

Raffles sniffed at the man's lips and then let the head fall back.

'Bitter almonds!' he muttered. 'Whilst we've been watching him, he has taken cyanide. He's dead, Bunny.'

CHAPTER TEN

A few hours later I sat opposite Raffles picking over a meal in the dining room of the Ritz Hotel. I had little appetite.

'I simply can't believe it,' I said for perhaps the hundredth time. 'I simply can't believe that a man would sit on a park bench and calmly take cyanide. It's unthinkable.'

Raffles grimaced as he helped himself to more oysters. The events of the afternoon had apparently not impaired his gourmet aspirations.

'Didn't I tell you, Bunny,' he grunted between mouthfuls, 'that all the best spies take poison rather than confess? Don't you read the adventures of Sexton Blake . . .?'

'Who?'

'That detective fellow in the *Union Jack* magazine.'

I looked at Raffles dumbfounded.

'You don't read that rubbish?'

'It's just as good as your *Strand* magazine with those awful cops and robbers stories written by that fellow Hornung. He's not very accurate, you know. In one tale he has a man escape from a bedroom window of Albany onto the top of a Hansom cab which happens to be driving by down a side street. Mister Hornung obviously knows little of the geography of Albany and he even talks about uniformed clerks showing potential residents over the apartments. Well, that's upset a few of the fellows I know who are resident there.'

'Well I happen to like Conan Doyle's Sherlock Holmes tales,' I countered defensively. The current June issue of the magazine contained a fascinating story entitled *The Three Students*.

'Those tales are all the same,' dismissed Raffles, pouring more wine.

'What now?' I asked after a suitable pause.

'While you were off telephoning Mackenzie, I searched the pockets of our friend Moltke. There was nothing on him except a little black notebook. In it there were a few jottings, mainly public transport times and the telephone number of the German embassy. There was one other entry . . .'

Raffles took the notebook from his pocket and pushed it across the table towards me. I scanned the pages.

'It doesn't say much,' I said. 'Just a date and a name.'

'On the contrary, Bunny,' returned Raffles. 'It says a great deal. The date, as you see, is Sunday, May 29. Just cast your memory back to a singular event on that date.'

I frowned, suddenly remembering Carson's words.

'Why, that is the date when the King's letters were stolen.'

'Exactly.'

'And the name here is Frank Sheehan. Do you suspect that this Sheehan was involved.'

'I'm sure of it. Sheehan is a name which is not unknown to me, Bunny. "Slippery" Sheehan has a reputation second to none as a cat-burglar. He's the best.'

I pulled at my ear, frowning.

'You think that Fuchs' group hired Sheehan to get the letters for them?'

'Why else would his name be entered so neatly and methodically against that particular date in Moltke's little black notebook. It's a slip which is greatly in our favour, Bunny.'

I sat back and whistled softly.

'You think Sheehan might lead us to Fuchs?'

'It's a better chance than trying to trace Fuchs through the other members of the network. What Moltke did, the others can do. Their profession is spying and they play for high stakes. Sheehan, on the other hand, is a professional criminal and will sell anything for a price – including information.'

Raffles glanced at his pocketwatch.

'I asked Mackenzie to join us here with information about Sheehan's last known address.'

As if on cue Mackenzie's stocky form pushed through the restaurant and slumped in a spare chair at our table. His face was dour. Raffles gestured to a hovering waiter.

'You'll join us for coffee, Mackenzie?' he asked, giving the order without waiting for a reply.

'I'll no object to that,' grunted the superintendent.

'Any further news about Moltke?' I asked.

Mackenzie shook his head.

'Poisoning by potassium of cyanide, says the doctor. Obviously suicide.'

'The facts have not been released to the press?' Raffles queried.

Mackenzie waited while the waiter came up with the coffee.

'As you requested, Mister Raffles, no report of the affair will be made public until you say so.'

'Good.' He sipped his coffee. 'Now, did you find out about Frank Sheehan's address?'

Mackenzie nodded.

'Aye, but I'm not sure I know what "Slippery" Sheehan has to do with this.'

Raffles leant back, took out a Sullivan and lit up.

'I think I know where that particular gentleman was on the night of May 29.'

Mackenzie's jaw dropped.

'You mean it was Sheehan who broke into . . .?'

'That's my guess,' affirmed Raffles.

Mackenzie started to rise from the table.

'I'll get out a warrant right away . . .'

'Sit down, Mackenzie!' Raffles gave the order quietly enough but it was enough to make Mackenzie slump back in his seat. 'Do you want to blow the whole game? We want Sheehan to lead us to Fuchs. Now, give us his address.'

Mackenzie hesitated and then passed over a piece of paper.

'He's a convict on licence. If I recall aright he was released at the beginning of May after doing a three year stretch in Strangeways. He lives in a tenement house in Salmon Lane, Limehouse.'

Raffles smiled.

'Excellent! Let's go and pay a call on Mister "Slippery" Sheehan, Bunny. No time like the present.'

'Shall I come with you?' asked Mackenzie.

Raffles shook his head.

'We'll probably need you later, Mackenzie. A private talk is the best thing at this moment.'

'What if he won't talk?' I demanded.

Raffles blew a series of smoke rings.

'The only thing that worries me is if Sheehan *can't* talk,' he said with emphasis.

We left Mackenzie fretting in the foyer and took a Hansom from the rank outside the Ritz. The cabby's eyebrows raised when we told him our destination.

'There'll be a guinea for yourself if you wait for us at the other end,' Raffles assured him.

'Right you are, guv'nor,' sighed the man reluctantly. 'But take my word for it, the Commercial Road ain't quite the place for gennelmen to be abroad at night.'

75

Having thus admonished our foolhardiness, he set his horse into a smart trot through the West End, heading through the City, crossing Aldgate into the Commercial Road. We were soon in Stepney and, after a while, came to the Docklands of London's East End. A short distance from a sign announcing Regents Canal Dock, the cabby drew into the curb and halted.

'Salmon Lane, guv'nor,' he said, pointing with his whip.

Raffles flicked him a coin.

'I see a pub on the next corner, cabby. We'll join you there as soon as our business is over.'

The driver knuckled his forehead and drove on.

'And now for "Slippery" Sheehan,' smiled Raffles.

I peered round in disgust. I had always thought that the East End of London was a foreign country; a dirty, squalid, overpopulated warren of narrow, disreputable lanes, lined on both sides with cheap lodging houses or dirty tenement blocks. It was late at night but the streets were still crowded with brawling, drunken men and women, arguing with degrading blasphemies. The vapours which rose from the sewer-like gutters were nauseous. I hardened my face and followed Raffles down the dark lane.

One or two women called out to us from shadowy doorways offering their *wares* in a most blatant fashion. I was blushing violently by the time we halted before a dirty house which made the Moreton Place tenement seem like a palace in comparison.

Raffles pushed at the door. It creaked open and emitted such foul odours that I found myself coughing. Undeterred, Raffles went in and stood in a dingy hallway lit by a flickering gas lamp whose unkept mantle was unable to provide an adequate light.

Raffles drew out a box of matches and lit one.

There were no signs on the doors so Raffles knocked loudly on the first one he came to. There was a faint sound of a chair scraping, a muttered cursing from a male voice and then the door opened, allowing a light from the room beyond to fall into the hallway. A stocky, red faced

76

man in a dirty vest and labourer's trousers glowered at us.

'Where can I find Frank Sheehan?' asked Raffles.

The man spat onto the floor between us. I moved uncomfortably aside.

'Sheehan, is it? Top floor, back room.'

The door slammed.

Raffles led the way up the creaking stairs until we finally came to a narrow landing. There were only two doors and Raffles rapped on the one which obviously led to the back room.

There was a few moments silence and then the door creaked slowly open about six inches.

The face that peered out with such hostility had once been pretty. Now it was ugly with eyes that were red from weeping, lips that were distorted with grief. The bright red hair was awry. The face of the women could have been any age between twenty-five and fifty-five.

'What d'youse want?' demanded the female apparition in a voice whose harsh accents identified it as northern Irish.

'I want a word with Frank Sheehan,' replied Raffles, making an effort to pull himself together before this harpie.

The woman stared in surprise and looked from one to the other of us for some seconds. Then, to our surprise, her face cracked into a grin. It made it seem even uglier. She threw back her head and gave a bellow of hysterical laughter.

'Youse want t'speak to Frank, is it?'

She began to giggle uncontrollably for some time while we looked on not knowing how to react. Then, abruptly, her face became serious.

'Bloody peelers, aint youse?'

'No, Mrs Sheehan,' Raffles assured her. 'It is Mrs Sheehan, isn't it? No, we aren't the police but we are connected with the Government.'

'Peelers! Government men! All the bloody same!'

She stared at us, her jaw thrust out aggressively.

'So youse want t'see my Frank, eh?'

77

Raffles nodded.

'Well youse just a wee bitty late. A wee bitty too bloody late!'

Raffles glanced at me in concern.

'I'm not understanding you, Mrs Sheehan,' he said slowly.

The woman swung back the door.

The room beyond was lit by two candles. In the centre of the room stood two kitchen chairs. Balanced on them was a plain deal wood box . . . a coffin. The lid was off and in it lay the body of a man.

Two old pennies covered his eyes. The smell of camphor was overpowering.

'That's what I mean!' cried the woman bitterly. 'Frank Sheehan is dead!'

CHAPTER ELEVEN

Raffles looked at the body for a long while and his shoulders perceptibly slumped.

'When did it happen and how?' he asked in a quiet voice.

Sheehan's wife was fighting to control her tears.

'This morning. He'd just gone down the road to the pub. Two neighbours brought him home. They said it was an accident. A coach came racing round the corner and ran him over . . . it drove on, it didn't stop.'

There was a dangerous tremor in her voice.

'The coach didn't stop?' Raffles' voice was sharp.

The woman shook her head.

'Look, Mrs Sheehan,' Raffles' tone was kindly. 'I must ask you a few questions about Frank. We know he was involved in a certain job on Sunday, May 29. Did he speak to you about it?'

The woman stared at Raffles, anger showing through her tears.

'So what?' she demanded. 'He's dead now, isn't he? Are you going to charge his corpse?'

'No, Mrs Sheehan, but – let me be brutal – Frank was hired to do a job. It might be . . .' he paused, 'it might be that those who hired him had a hand in his death. That this accident was rigged to prevent him from talking.'

Mrs Sheehan's eyes went wide.

'Jesus, Mary and Joseph!' she exclaimed. 'I told him not to have a hand in it . . . told him!'

She bit her tongue as she realised her confession.

'Go on, Mrs Sheehan,' prompted Raffles. 'Whatever you say will be treated in confidence. The police won't be involved, I promise you.'

She bit her tongue.

'Are you not peelers, then?'

'I told you, we are not but we work for the Government.'

Mrs Sheehan sniffed.

'What's in it for me? My man's dead. I've a wain to take care of and me with no friends in this godforsaken city. Is it good for the price of my fare back to Derry?'

Solemnly Raffles took out his pocket book and drew out one of the new five pound notes.

'There's another for you if you tell us everything.'

I wondered whether he would have to account to Mackenzie for making free of Government money in such a fashion.

Mrs Sheehan drew her shawl round her shoulders and went to sit in a rocking chair near the coffin. She gazed on the face of her dead husband for a moment and then sighed.

'Frank came out of Strangeways only four weeks ago. It was impossible for him to get a job. No way of going straight. Anyway, he was a damned fine second storey man, they say. One evening, about two weeks ago, a man came to the door . . . a foreigner.'

'A foreigner?' I interjected. 'A German?'

'God knows, they're all the same to me,' replied Mrs Sheehan.

'Can you describe him?' pressed Raffles.

79

Mrs Sheehan did so. It was a fairly accurate description of Moltke.

'What did they talk about, presumably he came to see Frank?'

Mrs Sheehan nodded. 'I didn't hear. Wasn't I trying to feed the wain at the time?'

I had only just reasoned out what a 'wain' could be, realising as she nodded to a small baby cot in a corner of that dreary room.

'The two of them went to the pub. When Frank came back he told me that he had a job and gave me five pounds there and then. The foreigner had hired him to break into a house up West somewhere. The only thing the foreigner wanted was a package of letters. Frank said that the man would pay him twenty-five pounds for them and he could keep any other valuable items he cared to lift.'

She paused and blew her nose.

'Frank went up West to scout the job. The foreigner had given him a plan of the house and exact details as to where the letters could be found. When Frank came back he was worried. It wasn't the type of place one man could do. He had to have a look out man. He didn't know where to contact the foreigner because the man had arranged to contact him after the job was done – a certain day had been arranged for the job. So Frank went ahead and hired his own man, reasoning that the silver plate he would pick up would cover the extra cost.'

Raffles nodded.

'And then?'

'The day fixed for the job was Sunday. It went smoothly. Frank got the letters and about three hundred quids worth of silver plate . . . only the fence gave him fifty quid the lot.'

She grimaced.

'He met up with the foreigner a few days later and handed over the letters. And did I see any of the money? No! That big Dublin bowsie went straightway to the races and blew the lot within two days! Now here am I with just enough money to pay for his interment.'

Raffles slowly laid down another note.

'Frank found out where the foreigner lived, didn't he?'

He asked the question softly, keeping his hand on the note.

'What d'you mean?'

There was a hint of fear in Mrs Sheehan's voice.

'Didn't Frank tell you that he had seen the foreigner who had hired him within the last couple of days and that, as he had blown the proceeds of the deal, he was going to attempt to put the black on the man for more money?'

I gaped; how did Raffles know this?

Mrs Sheehan gave a sob.

'Frank wasn't a blackmailer, mister.'

'You're right,' retorted Raffles. 'He should have stuck to second storey work. I think he paid dearly for trying to put the black on his former employer.'

The woman raised a hand to her open mouth and looked from Raffles to me with fear.

So that was it! My mind was slowly putting together the pieces from the conversation we had overheard in the German Embassy. *Der Erpresser* – the blackmailer – whom Fuchs had ordered to be eliminated, was Frank Sheehan. Sheehan must have spotted Moltke on the street, maybe followed him to his room and tried to blackmail him for more money. Sheehan had not realised what he was taking on. While Moltke was carrying out Fuchs' order and eliminating Sheehan, we had actually been searching Moltke's rooms. With his quick thinking Raffles had pieced it all together.

'Just one more question,' went on Raffles relentlessly, 'I want the name of the man who did the job with Frank. And I want to know where he can be found.'

'You can't ask me . . .' she began to protest.

'I can and will. If you tell me I'll not report anything of what you have said to the police. And I suggest, after you have buried your man, that you take the next train to Liverpool and get the boat to Belfast.'

She stared at him angry for the moment.

'His name is MacCreedy,' she finally said, softly. 'He's known as Tiny MacCreedy and he hangs out at the Rose

Thorn, the pub at the end of the street here.'

'Excellent. Oh, one more thing, Mrs Sheehan . . . do you know if MacCreedy was party to the blackmail?'

Mrs Sheehan shook her head.

'It was all Frank's idea, God look down on him!'

'Did Frank tell the foreigner that MacCreedy was in on the job.'

'I can't be sure. Now haven't I told you enough?'

'Indeed you have. Remember what I told you, Mrs Sheehan. London is proving unhealthy at the moment. A long holiday in Ireland is an excellent suggestion.'

Outside in the street I was bursting with excitement.

'So it was Moltke who hired Sheehan? But how did you put the facts together and come up with the idea that Sheehan was blackmailing Moltke?'

'It seemed a logical conclusion,' replied Raffles airily, as he led the way to the pub at the corner of the street.

The Rose Thorn was a rather dreary little pub, one of those *spit and sawdust* affairs. It was crowded and so filled with smoke that it was almost impossible to see across the room. The noise nearly drowned out one's thoughts. Above the hubbub a fiddler was striving, valiantly, to squeak out some folk tunes. There was no lounge bar but there was a little partitioned section labelled *The Snug*. We pushed our way into it.

'Evenin' gennelmen, what'll it be?' greeted the heavy jowled barman.

'Two pints of your best bitter and the answer to a question,' Raffles responded.

The man's eyes narrowed. He said nothing as he started to pour the beer.

'Is Tiny MacCreedy in here tonight?'

The man's eyes flickered momentarily in the direction of the public bar. The movement was not lost on Raffles.

'Excellent. Would you ask Mister MacCreedy to join us for a drink?'

'Police?' scowled the barman, realising it was fruitless to deny MacCreedy's presence.

'No.'

The barman shrugged and moved off along the bar.

'Tiny!' we heard him calling, bellowing above the noise. 'Gennelmen in *The Snug* want to buy you a drink.'

MacCreedy came through the partition, suspicion on his pug-face. It was obvious why he was called Tiny. He must have stood six foot three in his stocking feet.

'What d'youse want with me?'

He was a red faced man with blue eyes and ginger hair and the soft burr of a southern Irish accent.

The landlord pushed a pint of porter at MacCreedy and swept up the coins that Raffles had laid on the bar counter.

Raffles waited until the man had gone to serve someone else.

'A word, Mister MacCreedy. And, before you ask, no, we are not the police.'

'What d'youse want a word about?' MacCreedy asked pointedly.

'You've heard what happened to Frank Sheehan?'

The big man nodded.

'God be merciful to that ould skin,' he muttered and took a pull at his beer.

'We know you and Frank pulled a job on Sunday, May 29,' Raffles went on blandly.

MacCreedy blinked stupidly, his mouth hung open.

'If you ain't the polis, where d'you get that from?'

Raffles smiled.

'That's no concern of yours, Mister MacCreedy,' he replied evenly. 'Believe me, we know. Did Sheehan tell you he was putting the black on the man who hired him to do the job?'

This time MacCreedy spilt some of his beer as he jerked in surprise.

'Why, the two-faced bowsie!' he gasped. 'He never told me, mister. That ain't good in our business. Gives an honest man a bad name.'

Raffles smiled thinly.

'Sheehan seems to have paid for the error.'

MacCreedy turned white and took a step backwards, looking from one to the other of us with wide staring eyes.

'You mean, you . . . did you . . .?'

'No. We were not your erstwhile employers,' Raffles replied. 'And we did not kill Sheehan. Nevertheless, we know who did and we are interested in meeting up with them. Did Sheehan ever talk to you about the people who hired him?'

'God be my witness, sir, I never knew who hired him. Frank got the commission and then asked me to help him out. I don't know anything except Frank said that it was some foreigner who did the hiring. I asked no questions. It's better that way.'

Raffles stared into MacCreedy's face for a time and then nodded slowly.

'If I were you, MacCreedy, I'd make myself scarce for a week or two. If the people who killed Sheehan found out that you were working with him then your life wouldn't be worth much.'

MacCreedy nodded.

'I'm obliged to youse,' he said turning slowly into the public bar.

I followed Raffles from the pub feeling a little deflated.

'I was afraid it would lead to a dead end,' confessed Raffles. 'Even if Sheehan had still been alive, he could only have identified our late unlamented friend Moltke. It seems that Fuchs is rather a clever fellow and does not reveal himself to his underlings. It is going to be tough to track him down.'

'He's not only clever,' I observed, 'but he's dangerous. So far as we know, he has had two men killed and instilled such fear into his own people that they prefer to commit suicide rather than get caught and risk betraying him.'

Raffles shrugged.

'Let's go and collect our cabby, Bunny, and get back to Albany. We have to think out our next move.'

CHAPTER TWELVE

We sat in Raffles' lounge sipping brandies.

'It looks to me as though we are back to square one,' I observed, trying to break the silence which had fallen since our journey back from the East End.

'Not quite, Bunny,' Raffles replied. 'So far, Fuchs isn't aware that we are looking for him nor that we know the identity of the others in his little spy network. We still have some advantage.'

'But surely Fuchs will know something is amiss when he finds out about Moltke?'

Raffles shook his head.

'Mackenzie is keeping all details of Moltke's death from the press until next week. So far as Fuchs is concerned, Moltke has simply disappeared. Even if Fuchs does find out anything, what would it prove? Moltke took poison? So what? We know, having followed the wretched man, that he did not contact Fuchs before he went to Ranelagh Gardens. Therefore Fuchs does not know we are on his trail.'

'Very well,' I assented. 'But how can we proceed?'

'We will have to return to our original idea and work on another member of Fuchs' group.'

'What about the time factor?' I asked. 'We only have a few more days until the letters are handed over to a courier and taken out of the country.'

'Every day counts, old chap,' replied Raffles blandly.

'Well, then, who shall we tackle next? There's only our friend von Heumann or the Baroness von Stalhein.'

'That's right. One of them must lead us to Fuchs.'

Raffles frowned and scratched at his nose.

'Which one, that's the question.'

'Von Heumann was always an idiot,' I ventured.

'I doubt whether von Heumann would be pleased to see us again after our little affair on the *Uhlan*. We treated him badly there and he never retrieved that pearl. That was one of my better efforts . . .'

'Which landed me in jail,' I muttered savagely, not having completely forgotten the outcome to the adventure.

Raffles eyed me reproachfully.

'You received your share of the proceeds, Bunny, plus some interest for the inconvenience.'

I flushed. Raffles always had the ability to make me feel churlish when, logically, I knew I was not at fault. However, it was true that he compensated me for my loss of freedom.

He poured two more brandies from his decanter.

'I doubt whether we shall be able to wring much out of von Heumann,' he contemplated. 'In point of fact, I'm sure we are overlooking something. Something keeps stirring in the back of my mind. Something someone said and I'm damned if I remember it.'

I looked at him in silence for a while and then, as he seemed lost in thought, I prompted:

'Then you mean we should work on the Baroness?'

He chuckled.

'Work on the . . . really, Bunny! Where do you pick up this form of English? The editor of *The Strand* must be rather an uncouth gentleman to let such an expression into print.' He paused. 'But you are probably right. I'll look up the Baroness in the *Almanack de Gotha*. There must be some way of approaching her, getting an introduction. We will have to be a little more subtle with her, Bunny. We will have to try a different approach than we did with Moltke.'

I shuddered at the remembrance.

'I simply can't believe a man would take poison,' I said.

'You are becoming a little repetitious, old thing,' murmured Raffles. 'Anyway, I think we should sleep on things. Come and have breakfast with me in the morning, Bunny, and I'll try to work out some course of action.'

I rose to my feet reluctantly.

There were times when Raffles' nonchalant attitude drove me to utter distraction.

I was halfway back to Lord Toby Devenish's house when I realised that I had not chastised Raffles for the unspeakable way he had treated me in the Moreton Place tenement house that afternoon. He could have allowed me to be killed by his selfish action. What if Moltke *had* had another pistol secreted away on his person? I shuddered. Yet it was Moltke who lay dead, killed by his own hand while sitting on a park bench in the pleasant afternoon June sunshine. It all seemed so stupidly unreal.

My brother-in-law, Lord Toby, was sitting in the library with a cigar and brandy when I entered.

'Harry, old fellow,' he greeted. 'My you're a late bird. Haven't seen much of you in recent days.'

'I've been spending some time at my club,' I countered, feeling a little wary lest he should have found out that I had been an unwilling guest at Scotland Yard. I shuddered at the thought of Alice discovering the affair. Lord Toby waved a languid hand towards the decanter and so I helped myself to a drink.

'Heard from Alice lately?' he asked.

I shook my head.

'She's still in Paris, staying with her friends.'

He nodded, scratched his chin and cleared his throat – a little awkwardly I thought. For a wild moment I thought he *knew*.

'Look here, Harry, you know you are perfectly welcome to stay here as long as you like and all that, but I think I'd better warn you that I shall be leaving tomorrow for the weekend. I'm going down to Hurstdevenish . . . got a weekend party organised.'

Hurstdevenish was Lord Toby's country estate near Horsham in Sussex. I had stayed there several times with Alice.

I felt relieved. He didn't know about my arrest. I couldn't bear it if the story got back to Alice even though I had now redeemed myself by working for the Government.

'That's alright, Toby,' I replied. 'If you want, I can move into my club for the weekend.'

He waved his hand rebukingly.

'I wouldn't hear of it, old chap. Tell you what, though, why don't you come and join us? Lots of interesting people going to be there and we are having a cricket match on the Sunday – guests versus a village team. Should be tremendous fun.'

'I'm sure it would,' I smiled, 'but I do have some pressing business in town.'

'Put it off, old boy. Put it off. A weekend's relaxation is a damned good thing, you know. Interesting people . . . Admiral Fisher is coming – the First Sea Lord, you know. Oh, and the German ambassador, Count von Wolff Metternich . . .'

I must have started in surprise because Lord Toby stopped his recitation and peered at me.

'Do you know him?'

'No,' I said, struggling with a memory. 'It's just that I saw his name in the newspaper the other day but I didn't realise you knew him.'

Lord Toby shrugged.

'I met Paul about '98 or was it in '99 when I was in the Foreign Service.'

I recalled that Toby had been attached to our Berlin embassy some years ago when he was in the diplomatic corps, a position from which he retired on inheriting his title.

'Paul von Wolff-Metternich is a stout fellow. Became ambassador here the same year I decided to leave the Foreign Service. I think that was 1901 or was it '02. No, I tell a lie. It was 1901. We've kept in touch ever since. Anyway, where was I? Ah yes. Paul will be coming this weekend.'

Lord Toby drew a paper from his pocket and scrutinised it.

'I must remember the numbers,' he muttered. 'Deuced nuisance, you know, if the numbers don't tally. There's Paul and his countess, two aides, and another lady . . . Baroness von Stalhein. There's Lord and Lady Fisher and . . .'

He rambled on, listing the number of guests but I did not hear. Luckily his eyes were on the paper otherwise he would have seen my face working. The memory which had gnawed at Raffles' mind and which he could not recall now flooded back to me.

The Baroness von Stalhein had asked Fuchs if the weekend was still arranged. Fuchs had replied:

'The party? Yes, we shall all be there. It will be a unique opportunity to pump the old British sea-dog for information. But that will be the last time we gather together.'

The old British sea-dog! Lord Fisher – the First Sea Lord! Who else?

It was Lord Toby's party that they had been referring to. What a heaven sent opportunity! Fuchs would be at that party!

I had difficulty controlling my voice, so great was my excitement.

'I say, Toby,' I interrupted him, trying to make my voice sound casual. 'You know, perhaps you are right. I wouldn't mind getting away from London this weekend.'

'Delighted to have you, old boy,' breezed Toby.

'I could clear up my business and come down at lunchtime on Friday.'

'Jolly good. I'll put you down for the cricket match on Sunday. You know something about the game?'

I let the jibe pass.

'There is one thing though, Toby,' I said hesitantly. 'I had arranged to meet an old friend of mine, a brother officer from the Boer scrap and all that. Would it throw your figures out if he came with me? He's a good sort, old school chum and that.'

Lord Toby frowned over his list.

'Is he a cricket man?'

I nearly restrained myself from boasting of Raffles prowess and revealing that Raffles had taken the field many a-time for the English side.

'He's a very good man,' I assured him. 'In the school First Eleven.'

'Jolly good,' smiled Toby. 'By all means ask him down. We need an extra chap to make up the guests' eleven. The Germans don't play; don't really understand the game so there won't be much point in asking them to make up the team, if you get my meaning. Thought I was going to have to ask one of the servants to make up our eleven. That would have been a bit *infra dignum*; frightfully so, in fact . . . after all, the match is supposed to be guests versus villagers. Well, that really is splendid Harry, old fellow. I'll be delighted to see you and your friend down at Hurstdevenish on Friday.'

The next morning I could scarcely contain my excitement as I burst into Raffles' rooms and found him, clad in his revolting maroon smoking jacket, and poring over the *Almanack de Gotha.*

'You're abroad early, old fellow,' he greeted me. 'I'd better organise breakfast.'

'I've got some spiffing news, Raffles,' I blurted.

Raffles raised an eyebrow.

'Then spill it, old bean.'

'I know where Fuchs is going to be this weekend.'

Raffles stared at me with curiosity.

'Remember? When we were in the German Embassy we overheard them talking about a party this weekend? Fuchs said he was going to be there to pump information from an old British sea-dog.'

Raffles clicked his fingers.

'Of course! That was what I was trying to remember last night! I knew there was something we had overlooked. Marvellous that you remembered it, Bunny. But now we have to find out where.'

'I know where,' I announced, pushing my chest out. 'The party is a weekend party being held by my brother-in-law.'

Raffles whistled.

'What a coincidence! How did you learn this?'

Briefly, I told him of my conversation with Lord Toby.

'Splendid!' cried Raffles. 'You did well, Bunny old top. We will have to be on our toes, observe carefully every person Lord Fisher gets into conversation with and keep an eye on the Baroness.'

I preened myself a while as Raffles praised me for this development.

'And we go off to Hurstdevenish tomorrow morning?' he asked.

I nodded.

'It won't leave us much time,' he reflected, as he went into his kitchenette and busied himself preparing a breakfast.

'What do you mean?' I asked, following him.

'Just that the letters could be handed over as early as Monday. Fuchs said that it would be after the weekend. We must make sure we trap both Fuchs and the letters this weekend.'

He started to butter some toast.

'You'll find a Baedeker Railway Timetable on the sideboard, Bunny. Just check the times of the trains to Horsham, will you, old chap?'

I thumbed through the timetable.

'We can get a train at eleven-thirty tomorrow from Victoria,' I said. 'It will land us in Horsham within the hour. Incidentally, Raffles, do you still have your cricket whites?'

He frowned at me.

'Why?'

'I've volunteered our services to play in a guests versus villagers cricket game on Sunday which Toby has organised.'

'Lor',' murmured Raffles. 'I haven't played in an age. I'd better send out my togs for cleaning.'

We sat down to a breakfast of hot coffee, buttered toast and fruit preserves.

'What shall we do until tomorrow?' I asked.

'I don't know about you, old chap, but I shall be taking things easy. There's absolutely nothing we can do.'

'Oh,' I said.

I must have looked disappointed.

'There's no use wasting energy, Bunny,' admonished Raffles. 'Still, if you want to do something, I suggest you call in at New Scotland Yard and see Mackenzie. Tell him our plans for the weekend. He ought to get himself or a man down at Hurstdevenish and take up residence nearby.'

I nodded.

'Is Hurstdevenish on the telephone system?' Raffles suddenly asked.

'So far as I recall.'

'Good. We will probably need Mackenzie's help before the weekend is over.'

His words, though spoken at the time in a lighthearted vein, were to prove rather prophetic.

CHAPTER THIRTEEN

The journey to Horsham was without incident. As arranged Raffles and I met in front of Smith's bookstall at Victoria Railway Station. We purchased our tickets and summoned a porter to take our baggage to a compartment and settled down for the journey which took the best part of an hour. Horsham is one of those sleepy Sussex market towns, though the advent of a swift train service to London is sharply changing its way of life. Many City businessmen are purchasing houses in the environs of the town, travelling to London in the morning, enacting their business and returning in the evening. It is certainly not my idea of a gratifying lifestyle but, so Lord Toby says, one day this *commuting* will apply to the majority of people who work in the City. Our train drew into Horsham station at 12.31.

As we were climbing out and looking round for a porter an elderly man with grizzled grey hair and a smiling weather beaten face approached.

'Mister Manders, isn't it sir?'

'Charles?' I replied, recognising the man. 'You're Lord Toby's man?'

Charles raised a finger to his forelock.

'His Lordship's groom, sir. I've been sent to pick you and your guest up and to take you to the hall.'

Hurstdevenish has always been referred to as *the hall* by the locals.

'That's damned decent of Lord Toby,' I exclaimed. I had been wondering how we were going to complete the six mile journey from Horsham to Toby's estate.

Charles gathered up our baggage as if it weighed only a pound or two and preceded us through the red brick station building into the yard. Outside was a pony and trap, the type commonly known as a governess's cart. It was just large enough for Raffles and I to sprawl at our ease by our bags while Charles seated himself, flicked the whip over the pony's ears and set the cart lurching down the cobbled roadway.

The sun was strong, its rays flickering through the overhanging green boughs which canopied the roadway. It had a soporific effect and Raffles stretched, yawned and closed his eyes. We were soon out of the town and trotting through St Leonard's Forest and the little hamlet of Mannings Heath which led out towards Hurstdevenish. It was a brilliant early summer day with not a patch of cloud in the sky.

The red brick towers of Hurstdevenish rose to meet us as soon as we traversed a small knoll and swept around the shoulder of a wooded hill. The great house had originally been built in Tudor times. In fact, I believe it had been erected during the reign of Henry VIII for the house is laid out in the form of the letter 'H', a pretty compliment to the monarch. During the last unhappy years of Charles I the then Lord Devenish held it for the royalist cause and one wing of the house was destroyed by the artillery of a rather enthusiastic Parliamentarian officer. A generation passed before the building was repaired and the two distinctive Stuart towers were added. It was a large house, completely surrounded in its own parklands. I believe the famous English landscape gardener, Capability Brown, had a hand in laying out its sweeping gardens, lakes and woods. So far as I recall, Lord Toby had to employ eight full time staff to take care of the grounds alone.

Beyond the house itself was an area of woodlands and

hills which afforded a splendid reserve during the shooting season. Lord Toby's parties had been frequented by the King himself, when he was Prince of Wales. Beyond the woodlands, nestling in a small valley, was the little village which took its name from the family home of the Devenishes. The village lay about three-quarters of a mile from the house. It was a close-knit farming community which numbered scarcely more than a hundred souls.

'That's Hurstdevenish, Raffles,' I said, nudging him.

Raffles blinked, yawned and peered forward.

'Lor', Bunny, but that's a vulgarly large pile for one man to own,' he reflected.

Charles directed our pony and trap through the lodge gates and down the meandering drive which led through the parkland, passing ornamental lakes and rockeries to the sweeping lawns and front door. Toby's butler, Tomkins, was already standing there flanked by two uniformed footmen.

As Charles halted the pony and trap, Lord Toby came out to greet us.

'What ho, Harry!' he boomed.

I climbed down and began to introduce Raffles under his *nom de guerre*.

'Roberts, eh?' queried my brother-in-law. 'Roberts? Not one of the Petersfield Roberts – Lord Blane's lot?'

Imperturbably, Raffles assured him that he was not so related.

'Just as well, just as well,' grinned Toby, as he oversaw the unloading of our bags. 'Bad blood in that family. Bad blood.' Then he turned a serious face to me. 'Glad you're here, Harry. After you've had a wash and brush up can you help me out for a bit? Tell you the truth, Reggie Tew is here. Drat the fellow, but I had to invite him. Duty and all that rot. But the beastly man is getting in my hair. Do me a favour and see if you can head him off for a few hours to give me time to get things organised.'

I knew the Honourable Reggie Tew of old. If ever anyone inaugurates a prize for first class bores Reggie Tew would win it hands down. The man was a perfect menace, seizing anyone to hand and giving forth monologues on whatever happened to be his pet subject of that moment. To my certain knowledge three London clubs had requested his resignation from membership on the grounds that he was causing his fellow members to withdraw their membership because no one wanted to be buttonholed by Reggie Tew and bored into infinity.

I groaned audibly.

Lord Toby shot me a sympathetic look.

'Honestly wouldn't ask you to do this if I weren't desperate, old warhorse. I'll rescue you as soon as I am able. Promise. But I just had to have him down here. Tell you why later.'

'Very well, Toby,' I sighed.

He clapped me on the shoulder.

'Splendid show. Tomkins will show you to your rooms. See you later.'

Raffles and I followed Tomkins, the butler, through the great hall from whose stuccoed walls the frowning portraits of the tribe of Devenish glared down in varying degrees of disapproval. Suits of armour and all manner of medieval weaponry seemed to litter the place. Although I had stayed at Hurstdevenish several times with Alice, I was never really comfortable there; it was too much like camping in a museum.

We were shown to adjoining bedrooms in the north wing. As soon as I had washed, put on a clean shirt and made myself comfortable, I tapped on the adjoining door and entered. Raffles was combing his hair into place.

'What's the plan?' I asked.

Raffles gave a wry smile.

'For you it seems that the next couple of hours will be spent in the scintillating company of this Reggie Tew chap. Who is he?'

'A prize bore,' I wailed. 'A cousin of that revolting fellow Lord Amersteth.'

Raffles frowned for a moment, trying to remember.

'Amersteth? Of Milchester Abbey, Dorset, where we . . .?'*

* 'Gentlemen and Players' in *Raffles, The Amateur Cracksman.*

I nodded, preventing him from enlarging on a particularly embarrassing adventure involving the Dowager Marchioness of Melrose, a necklace of diamonds and sapphires and the unfortunate wounding of our old adversary Mackenzie who was then masquerading as a Mister Cleophane of Dundee.

'Yes, he's a pompous little ass. Sacked from Harrow, I believe but his family sent him off to some German university to round off his education. Halberstadt or somewhere.

Raffles eyes narrowed.

'A *German* university, you say?'

I caught his inflection and could not prevent myself from chuckling.

'Oh come on, Raffles. There's no need to suspect Reggie Tew of being Fuchs. The man's a first class clot.'

'Don't underestimate Fuchs. The character of a first class clot could be a splendid disguise. A German university is somewhat of a coincidence.'

'No more than the fact that Lord Toby worked in Berlin or that you and I can speak some German.'

'Lord Toby worked in the diplomatic corps in the British Embassy,' Raffles pointed out. 'And we can rule each other out as being Fuchs,' he added with undisguised sarcasm.

I stared at him in surprise.

'But Reggie Tew . . . no, I'll not believe that.'

'I'm not asking you to,' said Raffles. 'But don't simply dismiss it. Everyone is suspect this weekend.'

I was still reflecting on Raffles' preposterous suggestion when we went downstairs. Tomkins announced a light luncheon was being served in the dining room. There was only one person seated there. It was Reggie Tew.

Reggie Tew was a tall, lanky individual, with a shock of drab, colourless hair which, when he grew animated for any reason, fell straight across his forehead; the forehead was bulbous and I have heard some uninformed people pronounce that such a prominent forehead was a sign of intelligence. They had obviously not had the pleasure of

96

fifteen minutes in Reggie Tew's company. His pale and watery eyes stared through thick-lensed spectacles which balanced precariously on his gaunt cheeks.

'Manders, old chap!' his voice bordered on the falsetto. 'So you're down for the weekend, eh? Is Mrs Manders with you?'

I told him Alice was in Paris.

'Lucky for her,' he grunted, signalling to the waiter for soup. 'I'm sick to death of this country. Stupid politicians not knowing where they are going nor what they are doing. Politics are a joke here . . . look at that idiot Churchill. One day he claims to be a Tory and then the next he becomes a Liberal. How can you trust a politician? No wonder the country is in a mess. You can't tell one political party from another. The country needs strong leadership, a firm monarchy, an iron grip. What we want is a British Bismark . . .'

I took a deep breath and sat down next to him.

'Have you met my friend, A. J. Raf— er Roberts.'

Tew glanced up with a frown.

'Did he say Mister Ralph Roberts?'

'Roberts,' corrected Raffles blandly, shooting me a withering glance at my blunder.

'Delighted,' breezed Tew. 'Not a medical man, are you?' And before Raffles could disclaim the relationship, Tew pressed on: 'Know anything about this new thing for measuring heart contractions – an electro-cardiograph?'

Raffles managed to deny any knowledge.

'Just been invented by some German named Eintho-ven,' went on Tew oblivious of our lack of interest. 'Deuce clever people – the Germans. That's where the brains are in this day and age. I was working on a similar idea myself,' he chuckled with false modesty. 'Read medicine at Halberstadt. Never took my doctorate, though. Too interested in the mechanics of medicine ever to become a simple quack doctor. There's too much going on in the world to . . .'

Raffles pointedly asked for the bread.

As we finished the soup, progressed through a Quiche

Lorraine and salad, then through cheese, biscuits and coffee, Reggie Tew went blithely on stabbing at the air with his knife, fork and spoon at various times to make his points.

'Now what do you suppose the Frenchies are up to?' He suddenly asked *apropos* of nothing.

We looked at him blankly.

'This new Public Health Act of theirs,' explained Reggie. 'The reducing by law of the working day to nine-and-a-half hours! Smacks of Socialism to me? Mollycoddling the nation? Wouldn't be allowed in Germany. They'd know how to deal with things like that. Have I . . .?'

We groaned in unison as Reggie launched forth into another monologue on the marvels of that particular country.

I thought my head was going to burst. I will say this for Raffles, he stuck by me and each time I reached a point where I was going to throttle the loquacious Reggie, he stepped valiantly into the breach and saved me from that capital crime. Finally, as we were strolling in Lord Toby's conservatory at the back of the house, my brother-in-law came up bringing in his wake a large man who looked like a younger, stockier version of King Edward. He was a square headed man with a thick black spade beard, slightly balding but with thick eyebrows and an aggressive manner. He was dressed in a sombre black frock coat but his diamond and gold tie-pin and gold watch and chain marked him as a man of some substance in spite of the plainness of his dress.

'Forgive me for leaving you chaps alone,' said Lord Toby apologetically. 'I'd like you to meet Doctor Fyson, Doctor Seward Fyson.'

'Oh, I say!' it was a positive gurgle from Reggie Tew. 'You're not Seward Fyson who wrote the monograph on the Minnesänger language of German court poetry?'

Fyson bowed stiffly from the waist.

'I am acknowledged to be something of an authority on the ancient dialects of German.'

'Oh I say!'

Reggie only swallowed for breath before he was off.

'I have some new theories on the North German authorship of the manuscript known as *The Battle of the Goths and Huns . . .*'

Doctor Fyson looked politely interested. He had obviously never met Reggie Tew before.

'If you'll excuse us,' muttered Lord Toby, drawing us away. 'I must have a word . . .'

Reggie Tew and Fyson did not notice our departure.

'. . . and I believe the authorship is more Frisian than. . .'

'I'm damned grateful to you chaps,' smiled Lord Toby as we emerged from the conservatory onto the lawn. 'I had to invite Reggie, you see, because he is putting rather a lot of money into a business venture of mine . . . the Anglo-German Mining Corporation.'

'What's that Toby?' I asked, not having heard Toby mention this business interest before.

'Diamonds, Harry old chap. We are setting up a company to exploit some of the fields in German South West Africa. Actually, that's the real reason behind the weekend party. Everyone who is coming, saving yourselves, and old Admiral Fisher, of course, are thinking of investing some money into the venture.'

'Including Doctor Fyson?' asked Raffles.

'Yes. Fyson is a bit of a rum fellow but he has plenty of money to spare and he's chairman of the Anglo-German League. He could help smooth the path for the establishment of the corporation on German territory.'

'And the German ambassador is interested in the investment?'

Lord Toby looked horrified.

'Good Lor' no. I didn't mean to imply Count von Wolff-Metternich was taking a business interest. No; but he, as an old friend of mine, is willing to give advice. To be truthful, it helps to have influential friends to pull a few strings, if you see what I mean.'

'Has he arrived yet?' I interrupted.

'The Count? No, should be arriving later on. He's coming down with his entourage by car. Hopes to get here for dinner. Incidentally, we dine at eight o'clock.'

'His entourage?'

'Well, the countess and their guest, Baroness von Stalhein and two aides.'

'I see. Who are the . . .'

There was a movement behind us and Lord Toby's face broke into a smile of welcome.

We turned to see a tall, elderly man coming across the lawn. He was in his early sixties. One had the impression of a mild mannered man, a man with the benevolence of a bishop, with soft blue eyes and a courteous manner. Although he was not in uniform, I had no difficulty in recognising John Arbuthnot Fisher, the new First Sea Lord.

'Devenish, thought I'd pay my respects as we've just arrived.'

Lord Toby pumped his hand and then introduced Raffles and I.

'Lady Fisher has gone to our room to, what is that American expression, freshen up? Yes, freshen up. I need a walk – that's my way of relaxing. When I was made a captain in 'Seventy-Four I had my third officer chalk out a deck area every morning before breakfast so that I could walk three miles to relax myself before commencing the day's chores.'

'Shall I come with you?' ventured Lord Toby.

'No, damn it! Have to be alone. By the way, when's our friend Metternich coming? Want to pump him about these new expansions to the German High Seas Fleet. Don't like it, Devenish. Don't like it one bit. Why else would the Germans be increasing the number of their capital ships for except to push our Grand Fleet off the high seas? Why else?'

The question was rhetorical for the First Sea Lord turned with a wave of his hand and marched off across the lawn.

Lord Toby sighed.

'I don't want to bring politics into the conversation this weekend. I'll call on you chaps to help me out. Promise that if you see things looking sticky step in and change the conversation. Politics are an infernal nuisance.'

'Still,' murmured Raffles, 'you always take a bit of a chance when you invite the British First Sea Lord and the German ambassador to the same house party, especially with things going the way they are in Europe.'

Lord Toby looked bewildered and shrugged.

'Never really understood politics. That's why I finally resigned from the Foreign Office. Never was my idea to go into it in the first place. Pater's idea, really. Said it would keep me out of mischief. Well, six years as a cultural attaché in Berlin was enough for me. The FO were glad to see me go – several *faux pas* credited to my account. Once mistakenly sat a German general next to the French mayor of Bapume who was visiting Berlin. All hell to pay.'

'Why was that?' I asked curiously.

'Seems the jolly old Boche general, when he was a captain, served in von Goeben's army in the Franco-Prussian War. When the Germans defeated the French at Bapume in 'Seventy-One, this chap was one of the garrison troop who took it out on the French civilians. Trouble was, the wretched Boche insisted on reminiscing during the serving of the cheese and biscuits. Total uproar, old warhorse! Nearly caused an international incident, all 'cos I sat 'em next to one another. I'll have to make sure I put everyone in the right place tonight.'

He grinned.

'Trouble is you never can tell . . . I don't know the ambassador's aides for example. One is the brother of the Baroness but the other is some colonel . . . what's his name? Von Heumann.'

I started and even Raffles turned a shade paler.

'Von Heumann?' I exclaimed.

'Yes. Do you know him? He's a military attaché or some such thing.'

Just then Tomkins approached and drew Lord Toby to one side to discuss some arrangements.

I turned a white face to Raffles.

'Of course, Fuchs said that they would *all* be at the party! The game will be up as soon as von Heumann sees us, Raffles. Six or seven years is not all that long. The wretched man will recognise us for certain and denounce us as the people who robbed him on the *Uhlan*.'

Raffles chewed his lips for some time before lowering his shoulders in a dejected fashion.

'I'm afraid you're right, Bunny.'

CHAPTER FOURTEEN

'Well,' I prompted as we walked across the lawns, 'what shall we do now — make some excuse and leave before the German ambassador and his party get here?'

Raffles shook his head violently.

'No, by the Lord Harry! We can't miss this opportunity to track down Fuchs.'

He stopped in mid-stride and suddenly grinned.

'I think it is about time that Mackenzie started to pull his weight in this little affair.'

I did not understand what he meant and said so.

'Devenish said that the ambassador's party were arriving by motor car, didn't he?'

'Yes.'

'Then, from what you say, there are only two roads by which they could approach Hurstdevenish. If we could get some of Mackenzie's uniformed men to stop the car with an urgent message for von Heumann asking him to return to the embassy, it would give us at least another day to hunt around for Fuchs without von Heumann interfering.'

I pursed my lips.

'But when von Heumann gets back to the embassy he will discover that he has been tricked.'

'Yes, but by whom? The police could blandly tell him they were mistaken. And by the time he returns to Hurstdevenish we might have accomplished our task. He couldn't return before tomorrow morning.'

I looked at my wrist watch.

'We'd better get hold of Mackenzie,' I said.

'You say that he is going to stay at the White Bull in the village under the name of Mister Cleophane of Dundee?'

'It seems to be his favourite pseudonym,' I commented.

'Well, it's a three quarter of a mile walk, you'd better get cracking.'

I bit my lips in annoyance. Raffles always seems to land me with the dirty jobs.

'Off you go, Bunny. Sharp's the word!' prompted Raffles.

With a deep sigh I turned and started off swiftly towards the roadway – hardly more than a narrow track, in fact – which led me towards the village. It was a good half-an-hour before I came down the knoll to the collection of cottages which constituted the village of Hurstdevenish. The village had grown up with the estate and once all its inhabitants worked on Devenish lands. But times had changed. The villagers were still primarily farm workers but were distributed among the other profitable small holdings in the surrounding countryside.

As I approached the old half timbered Tudor building which was the White Bull, I spotted my man at once. Mackenzie was sitting on a rustic wooden bench outside the public house, sipping a frothing pint of stout.

'Afternoon, Mister Cleophane,' I said cheerily as I took a seat beside him.

'What is it, Manders?' he returned brusquely. 'You're not supposed to know me,' he added *sotto voce*.

I reddened. Really, these spy games were beyond me.

'Never mind,' grunted Mackenzie, alias Mister Cleophane, 'we'll pretend we just met. What is it?'

I suppose one must forgive the poor fellow his rudeness. He had always been a thorn in our side when Raffles and I were on opposite sides of the fence. It must seem difficult to adapt to the new circumstances.

I briefly explained Raffles' suggestion.

Mackenzie scratched at his chin.

'Och, I dinna say I like it, but I'll awa' and do it for the sake o' the job. Though it's going to cause a deal of trouble when the man discovers he's been sent on a fool's errand.'

I clapped his shoulder in approval.

'Well done, Mackenzie,' I murmured. 'But the whole game is ruined if von Heumann spots us and recognises us.'

Mackenzie shot me a dour look.

'I'll arrange for motorcycle patrols to intercept the ambassador's car and they can give von Heumann a lift back to the railway station.'

I exclaimed as I had a sudden flash of inspiration.

'Your man can tell von Heumann that a Mister Moltke has asked them to contact him and request him to return to the embassy immediately. That will send him scurrying back to London in record time.'

Mackenzie smiled thinly.

'Will it now? Doesn't it seem strange that one spy contacts the police to ask them to inform another spy of a rendezvous?'

I hesitated.

'It might appear to von Heumann as a mark of the urgency of the situation,' I suggested.

'Mebbe so. All right, I'll do it. But I won't promise results.'

Mackenzie finished his stout, bade me good-day and went off into the White Bull. When he had gone I suddenly realised that he hadn't even offered me a drink and now I had to tramp back to the hall.

It took me longer to return to Hurstdevenish than on my outward journey. By the time I reached the hall several more guests had arrived whose introductions by Lord Toby I promptly forgot. The guests were seated on the verandah of the house tucking into strawberries and cream. I flopped on a chair next to Raffles and barely had time to indicate that my task was accomplished when the obnoxious Reggie Tew materialised at my elbow.

'Manders, old fellow, been looking for you.'

I groaned inwardly and helped myself to a large dish of

strawberries from Tomkins' proffered tray.

'You're a scribbler of sorts, aren't you. I have a really first class idea for a story . . . a detective novel, actually. I thought you might be able to give me a few pointers.'

I let Reggie's boring treble float over my head, grunting from time to time through my digestion of the strawberries and cream. Finally I became aware that Reggie's voice had stopped on an interrogative note and so I muttered a few words and gave him the name of a literary agent. It so happened that a few weeks before I had been at a literary function and had been introduced to Mister Rider Haggard's agent, Mister A. P. Watt, whose name I now made free of.

Tea was just finishing when we heard the noise of a car engine.

Lord Toby sprang up with a smile.

'This should be Count von Wolff-Metternich,' he said brightly and proceeded round to the front of the house.

Raffles signalled to me and we rose casually and followed him at a stroll, halting at a spot where we could observe the arrival of the new guests without being seen ourselves.

A large touring car, one of the biggest I had ever seen, snorted to a halt in front of the door of Hurstdevenish. A tall, upright figure, wreathed in travelling clothes climbed stiffly out.

'Paul, my dear fellow, how are you?' greeted Lord Toby.

The tall figure gave a stiff bow.

'Delighted to see you again, my dear friend.'

He turned and helped out a female figure, also wrapped in a grotesque travelling coat and hat, which totally obscured her identity, although her movements betrayed her as elderly.

'Permit me,' went on the Graf von Wolff-Metternich. 'You know my wife?'

Lord Toby bowed low over the countess's hand and muttered something which was not audible to us.

The count was turning and helping a second female figure out of the car, a slight figure and obviously younger than his wife. In her arms she carried a small yelping dog.

'And this is our guest, the Baroness von Stalhein.'

The driver had now extracted himself from the vehicle.

'And this is my aide, Leutnant Erich von Stalhein. The baroness's brother.'

There was some more bowing and handshakes before we heard Lord Toby say: 'But wasn't I expecting five of you . . .?'

'Ah yes,' replied the count. 'Oberst von Heumann had journeyed down with us. But a most curious thing happened. We were stopped on the road not too far from here by one of your policemen on those – what do you call them – *motorrad*?'

'Motorcycle,' supplied Lord Toby.

'Ah, just so. There was some urgent message at the embassy for his attention. The policeman offered him a lift back to the railway station in order not to interrupt our journey. Most kind. Most courteous. He sends his regrets but hopes to join us tomorrow.'

'Oh dear,' murmured Lord Toby. 'Such a bore for the fellow. Never mind. We hope to see him tomorrow, then.'

He ushered them inside as Raffles turned to me with a grin.

'Well done, Mackenzie, eh?'

I nodded and then a thought struck me which made me go cold.

'Raffles, the German embassy is on the telephone system. What if von Heumann thinks of telephoning the embassy before leaving Horsham.'

'Von Heumann was always an ass. He obviously hasn't done so or Mackenzie would have tried to contact us on Lord Toby's telephone . . .'

Just then, as if on cue, Tomkins the butler emerged from the side of the building and hailed Raffles.

'Ah, Mister Roberts, you are wanted on the telephone in the library. The gentleman says he is your legal adviser – a Mister Cleophane, sir.'

'Oh Gawd!' I muttered. 'I was right!'

Raffles frowned at me before following Tomkins into the study.

I was quaking in my shoes when he returned and prepared to set off to the village at a quick trot to avoid von Heumann but Raffles was smiling.

'It was only Mackenzie confirming that von Heumann had caught the train back to London. That fellow is developing a sense of humour in his old age – my legal adviser, indeed!'

I felt weak and made for a nearby wicker chair.

'Buck up, Bunny,' reproved Raffles. 'I told you von Heumann was a clot. We now have some time this evening to see if we can spot our man.'

That evening we gathered for dinner at a quarter-to-eight. I have attended many house parties in all manner of places but in that singularly august company I found myself struck with awkwardness. There were nearly two dozen guests; thirteen men, a number which seemed to put Lord Toby out as he had counted on fourteen with the presence of the absent von Heumann, and ten ladies. The prominent guests were Lord Fisher, the First Sea Lord, and Count von Wolff-Metternich, the German ambassador, with their respective ladies. Lord Toby's partner for the evening was Anna Doubrovska of the Imperial Russian Corps de Ballet. It was my belief that Lord Toby was somewhat soft on that particular lady for he had, to my certain knowledge, been attending the ballet fairly regularly though I am sure he detested that particular art form.

Among the other guests were the Liberal peer Lord Bellamy and his wife; the African explorer Captain Walker and Mrs Walker; and Sir Peter and Lady Lonsdale, reputed for their entrepreneurial enterprises. I could not understand why Lord Toby had invited them because they were a most boring couple. There was Lady Pellinore-Crudgett and her appalling daughter Augusta. I had a suspicion Lord Toby had worked it so that Reggie Tew could partner Augusta – they were certainly ideally suited. As the *apéritifs* were being served Reggie was lecturing her on his theories about German court poetry.

There was the financier Jason Sickert and his wife, attending presumably because of Lord Toby's new business enterprise. The ambassador's young aide, Erich von Stalhein, was engaged in conversation with Lord Fisher's flag-lieutenant, Lieutenant Symes. There was the rather strange Doctor Fyson and the absolutely stunning Baroness von Stalhein plus Raffles and myself.

Tomkins and some footmen ushered our party into a reception room where the pre-dinner drinks were being served. I must doff my hat to Raffles for his style. When we entered the Baroness von Stalhein was nursing a cocktail with a bored expression as she stood by her brother who was being forced to listen to Reggie Tew's pronouncement on 12th Century German court poetry. Raffles, seizing a whisky sour from a hovering footman, sailed into the party, introducing himself and, without apparent pre-intention, manoeuvred the Baroness away from Reggie and young von Stalhein. It was ably done.

I stood sipping my drink and observing them from the corner of my eye. Raffles had stated his intention to attach himself to the Baroness as she was the only person at the party whom we knew for sure was part of the spy network. Standing there, it was the first time – so I realised – that I had seen her properly. My first thought was an envy that I had not volunteered to take the job of keeping her company. My second thought was that it was strange how anyone so lovely could be part of a deadly spy ring. She was not more than twenty-eight and held herself with an upright poise. Her figure was excellent. Her hair was dark brown but glowed with a red tint when the light fell on it. She had a fairly high forehead and a slightly long face, although it was in perfect proportion. Her skin was cream coloured with a faint natural redness above the cheek bones. The mouth was delicate and seemed to smile naturally. Her dark eyes gazed up at Raffles in unashamed appraisal. I was jealous. The woman was undoubtedly beautiful. I felt a tinge of guilt as the thought of Alice interrupted these musings.

I was about to go across and introduce myself, for I did

not see why Raffles should have all the fun, when Lord Toby caught hold of me.

'Harry, dear fellow, I have a bit of a chore for you,' he said in a low voice with an apologetic smile. 'Can you take Augusta Pellinore-Crudgett into dinner when it is announced?'

I groaned.

'What about Reggie Tew?' I protested.

Lord Toby grimaced.

'Reggie is going to escort Lady Pellinore-Crudgett,' he explained, leading me to where the anaemic young daughter of that forbidding matriarch stood giggling in a falsetto voice. She turned and peered short-sightedly at me, blushed and giggled once again as Lord Toby introduced us. She was, according to the society column of *The Times*, due to make her first appearance in Society at the autumn débutante's ball, having just completed finishing school in Switzerland. I felt sympathy for the unsuspecting Society. Her sole contribution to any conversation seemed to be: 'Oh, I say!' and 'But really!' and emphatically 'Rather!' with punctuations from her falsetto giggle.

It seemed that Madam Doubrovska caught my look of desperation because she smilingly joined us and asked if I liked *the* dance? It was a few seconds before I realised that by *the* dance, Madam Doubrovska meant only one form of dance – Ballet. She was an angular woman, beautiful and as assured as any queen. Of course, in her field, she was the queen – the prima ballerina of the Imperial Russian Ballet.

I agreed nervously that I did indeed like *the* dance.

'Ah, dear boy,' she smiled benignly, 'did you see me dance in Mozart's *Don Juan*?'

My ignorance of ballet is colossal and, to be truthful, I have only gone to one performance in recent years. As chance would have it, it had been a performance of *Don Juan* and only because Lord Toby had given me a spare ticket. With some assurance I declared I had seen her and found her performance only outclassed by her beauty. It seemed a ridiculous thing to say but I knew these *artistes* tend to be vain and appreciative of such compliments. My speech was greeted with a falsetto giggle from Augusta. Madam Doubrovska favoured her with an ill-tempered frown but turned a beaming smile upon me.

'Ah, dear boy, you are a perceptive young man.'

Madam Doubrovska was scarcely older than me but she addressed every man as *dear boy* even Lord Fisher, whose face turned several shades of purple and who gurgled inarticularly at the epithet.

'You must come to see me dance again,' Madam Doubrovska was saying.

'I saw Karsavina dance when I was in Vienna,' ventured Augusta, obviously feeling it time to make some contribution to the conversation.

This drew an expression of scorn from Madam Doubrovska.

'Karsavina!' she proclaimed the name as if it were an oath. 'Karsavina! The woman is untalented, she will never rise from the Mariinsky Theatre, never become a great artiste. I, I Doubrovska,' (she hit her chest with a resounding thump which made me wince) 'I was prima ballerina at Mariinsky when Karsavina was a mere nothing! Nothing! I was dancing with Fokine when he was at his greatest. What is Fokine now but a second-rate choreographer? Have you seen the monstrosity he has created from Tchaikovsky's *La Dame de Pique*? Ugh! It is an insult, an insult to art!'

When Madam Doubrovska shuddered, she shuddered with her whole being.

At this point the dinner gong sounded and interrupted Madam's waxing eloquence.

Steeling myself, I offered Augusta Pellinore-Crudgett my arm and escorted her into the dining room. I found myself seated with Augusta on one side of me and Mrs Walker, the wife of the African explorer, on the other side. Raffles sat further along the table, on the opposite side between the Baroness and Lady Bellamy. He had evidently made a deep impression on the Baroness for the two of them were engaged in a conversation which kept up through the meal to the exclusion of everyone else.

On the far side of Augusta sat poor Lieutenant Symes who manfully tried to make conversation with the young lady. Throughout the soup and fish courses I kept hearing her intermittent 'Oh, I say!', 'But really!', 'Rather!' and her falsetto giggle.

'And what do you do, Mister Manders?' Mrs Walker asked as the main dishes were being served. 'Are you a gentleman of leisure?'

I thought desperately and then decided to tell part of the truth.

'I am a writer,' I said, trying to sound modest.

'Really? How interesting. My husband, the captain, has written two volumes about his safaris in British East Africa. Have you read them?'

I confessed I had not.

Mrs Walker smiled and leant close to me.

'To tell you the truth, neither have I. The captain can be so boring when he starts talking about Africa.'

I looked at her slightly shocked. She was sipping her wine not in the least concerned by her intellectual infidelity to her husband.

'What sort of writing do you do, Mister Manders?'

I admitted to some verses and essays into the realms of popular fiction. When pressed further I admitted to some tales of criminal detection and a ghost story which I had managed to get published in Mister George Newnes' *Grand Magazine*.

Mrs Walker clapped her hands with delight.

'Oh, I do so adore those sort of tales. I am just reading the most marvellous little tale in the April *Royal Magazine*. It's all about a statue that has been seized from a Hindu temple and now stands in the centre of an ornamental pond in an English town. The statue comes to life to revenge itself on the people who stole it. Oh, it is so exciting. It was called *The Goddess of Death*, I believe.'

As an avid reader of popular story magazines, I knew the tale in question. It appeared that Mrs Walker and I shared a taste for that type of literature and spent the rest of the meal discussing the merits of a weird novel entitled *The Mystery of the Sea* written by an Irishman who had previously made a reputation in that field with a mysterious spine-tingling novel called *Dracula*.

In spite of the deep interest which the conversation held for me, for Mrs Walker was witty, intelligent and rather attractive, I tried to keep an eye on Raffles and his progress with the Baroness. They were still deep in conversation and I was about to return my attention to Mrs Walker when I happened to catch sight of one of the footmen who was standing immediately behind Raffles and the Baroness. A casual glance would make a person think he was merely waiting for orders to clear the table or attend to the wants of his guests.

He was a gaunt looking, dark haired man, standing as though he were thoroughly out of place in his footman's uniform and surroundings. Now and again he would run a nervous finger around his collar as though it were too tight.

What made me give him a second look was his eyes. They were riveted on Raffles and the Baroness. His head was slightly to one side. It was obvious that the man was listening intently to all that was being said.

CHAPTER FIFTEEN

It was some time later in the evening that I was able to put a question to Lord Toby in a casual manner.

'That's not one of your usual servants, is it?' I asked, nodding in the direction of the suspicious looking footman. 'I don't seem to have seen him at Hurstdevenish before yet his face is oddly familiar.'

Lord Toby glanced with disinterest to where the man was serving drinks.

'Oh, that's a temporary chappie. We were short staffed this weekend and Tomkins had to hire some agency people. I think the man's name is Carter, no, Cartwright. That's the name.'

'Then I must have seen him at someone else's house.'

Just then Jason Sickert came up and button-holed Lord Toby about his new Anglo-German Mining Corporation. At once my brother-in-law became animated.

'. . . you see, in the area where we have purchased the concession, the action of the weather has loosened heavy minerals from the rocks that contained them. The action of flowing water has gradually swept away lighter material leaving concentrations of the heavier minerals in placer deposits. Basically, old chap, all one has to do is bend down and pick up the diamond bearing lodestones . . .'

I sighed and left them to it. We had moved into the drawing room to join the ladies who had previously made their ritual departure from the dining room while the cigars and brandy were passed round. Raffles, I noticed, made a bee-line for the Baroness which seemed to please her. I must admit to an envy of Raffles' easy way with women; they all seemed to fall for him, his tall saturnine handsomeness, his charm and aura of mystery.

I looked round the drawing room. In a corner Lord Fisher was arguing some obscure points of naval law with the German ambassador. I think the conversation was turning dangerously political for it seemed to be about the future role of the new German High Seas Fleet and its growing conflict of interest with our own Grand Fleet. I saw Lieutenant Symes, Fisher's flag-lieutenant, and Leutnant von Stalhein, trying vainly to lighten the conversation of their superiors.

I paused to listen to the conversation of Captain Walker who was heatedly arguing with the dreadful Reggie Tew about German philosophy and the work of someone called Nietzsche who, judging by what Walker was saying, seemed to be rather scornful of humanity and morality though Reggie was making an ardent defence of the man.

I began to experience a feeling of helplessness. We were here to find out the identity of the master spy Fuchs. But he could be any one of the strange assortment of people gathered under my brother-in-law's roof. It seemed a hopeless task. I suddenly noticed that Raffles was surreptitiously signalling me and nodding towards the door.

A few moments later he joined me in the hallway.

'How are things going?' I asked, perhaps a little bitterly.

He ignored me.

'Listen, Bunny. I have a little job for you. Nip up smartly to the Baroness's room and have a poke around. See if you can find anything that will give us a lead.'

I opened my mouth indignantly.

'The Baroness's room,' went on Raffles, ignoring my attempt to protest, 'is in our wing. Three doors away from your room, in the same corridor. I'm going to keep her engaged for a little longer. Look smartish, Bunny, this might be our only chance.'

'Dash it, Raffles,' I managed to get in. 'This is not exactly in my line . . . oh, all right,' I said hastily, seeing his changing expression. 'But listen here. There's a footman who seems to be taking rather a particular interest in you and the Baroness. He's not one of Lord Toby's usual staff; he's hired for the weekend from an agency, name of Cartwright. You can't miss him – the chap looking uncomfortable and always hovering round you.'

Raffles' eyes widened.

'Well observed, Bunny. I'll keep an eye on him. Now you mention it, I did notice the man looking at me oddly once or twice.'

Raffles returned to the drawing room whilst I made my way unwillingly upstairs. I was not pleased at the prospect of acting the sneak thief in my brother-in-law's house. Still, I had to pull my weight in this strange affair.

No one was about as I entered the corridor where our bedrooms were situated. I gave a glance around and walked down the corridor to the end door, the third door from my own room. It was locked. Well, I was no locksmith and that put paid to the adventure. Surely Raffles would ask no more of me. I turned back to my room, entered and poured myself a glass of water. At once a nagging voice began to sound in my head. Raffles was doing his share of the work and expected me to do mine. It was not really playing the game to allow myself to be stopped by a mere locked door. Raffles would have overcome that obstacle without blinking an eyelid.

I perched myself on the end of the bed and tried to think it out.

We were on the third floor of the house and, if my memory was not playing tricks, under the windows of the third floor there ran an ornate structure which consisted of a ledge which encircled the whole house. I went to the window and opened it. Sure enough, a parapet about eighteen inches wide ran along under the window disappearing in the direction of the Baroness's room. Could I dare it? The drop to the courtyard was thankfully shrouded in blackness and therefore the actual height was obscured and did not trouble me.

Without pausing to think what I would do if the Baroness's windows were shut, I hoisted myself out onto the parapet, thinking how pleased Raffles would be with my exploit. There was no wind, something I should have been thankful for had my mind worked out the implications. With my face to the wall, my body spreadeagled against it, I managed to edge my way along without difficulty.

As everyone still seemed ensconced in the drawing room, no one was occupying the intervening rooms between mine and that of the Baroness so that I was able to pass freely by. Certainly luck was with me for when I reached the Baroness's windows they were standing slightly open. It was with comparative ease that I dropped into her room and stood to catch my breath.

I stood peering round, trying to judge my bearings, and then slipped my hand into my pocket to draw out the pencil flashlight which Raffles had taught me always to carry on my person. As I turned it on I heard a sudden movement and something gripped at my trouser leg.

A shocking yelping bark broke out.

I shone the beam down and found myself being snapped at by a rather repulsive looking animal, a dog with a sharp pointed face and an abundant white, creamy coat. It was, I believe, a *spitz* or Pomeranian breed who are notorious for being highly strung.

I cursed my memory. The Baroness had arrived carrying the tiny dog. I should have remembered and prepared for it. The noise of its petulant barking seemed to echo all over the house. I tried to pat it but it snapped at my hand with its tiny glistening jaws and I only just managed to snatch my fingers away. I tried speaking to it softly, reassuringly, so I thought, but the sound of my voice seemed to encourage it to go off into a further frenzy of yelping.

With a flash of inspiration I recalled that I had some toffees in my pocket which were not recommended for feeding dogs with but I was desperate. I unwrapped a couple and threw them at the animal. It stopped barking for a moment and regarded the toffees with a snarl of suspicion. Finally it licked at one, obviously liked the taste and snapped it up with a soft whimper. The beast's tail started to wag. I threw down some more toffees and by such means won that accursed animal's confidence and silence. Pausing only now and again to feed that creature's greed, I made a thorough search of the Baroness's belongings. There seemed no personal papers in her luggage nor any other items which would provide a clue to her involvement in Fuchs' spy ring.

I was thoroughly despondent as I finished a brief search of the Baroness's cosmetic box.

There was a movement at the door, a rattle of a key.

I froze.

'Are you sure you will be all right now, Baroness?' came Raffles clear voice.

'It is good of you to escort me but there was no need,' replied the softer tones of the Baroness. 'Good night, Herr Roberts; it has been a pleasurable evening.'

I turned with as much speed as I could summon, startling the wretched dog which suddenly let out an outraged yelp. Then I was out of the window and halfway along the ledge before you could say *Jack Robinson*. It was then that I realised that I had not adjusted the Baroness's windows properly. Well, I could not return then. I pressed on and was just crawling through the window in my room when Raffles opened the door and stared at me in amusement.

'Bunny, Bunny,' he shook his head reprovingly. 'If you are going to start any more nocturnal wanderings I suggest that you lock your door.'

Still shaking from my escape I poured myself a tot of brandy from my travelling flask.

'She'd locked the door so I had to get along the ledge and enter through the window,' I gasped, slumping into a chair.

'So I deduce, dear chap,' he said, sitting down and lighting up a Sullivan.

'Then there was her wretched dog. I'd forgotten all about it.'

'Any luck?'

'Not a thing. Not a bally clue. Nothing.'

'That's a pity.'

We sat silently for a while.

'What do we do now?'

'Press on. I've promised to take the Baroness riding tomorrow morning. Do you know that she's not really German. She's Austrian. Rather an intelligent young lady.'

I noticed a wistful look in his eyes.

'Well don't forget, Austrian or not, she's spying for the Kaiser.'

'Yes,' he said shortly and stood up. 'Anyway, we know Fuchs is here and his job is fairly easy by my reckoning.'

I frowned.

'What do you mean?'

'Fisher, the First Sea Lord, is a nice enough fellow but he does like to hear himself natter. Oh, he's careful enough when the Germans are about. He avoids particularising on information that would prove useful to them. But I overheard him just now jabbering away about the Grand Fleet to that ass Reggie Tew. He was sailing pretty close to the wind in describing the role of the Grand Fleet in blockading German sea ports in the event of a war.'

'Talking to Reggie Tew?' I laughed. 'Surely you're not still suspicious of that dunderhead, are you?'

'I'm suspicious of everyone,' returned Raffles evenly.

'Oh hang it, Raffles! Reggie Tew! I *say*!'

'Look, Bunny, just consider the people in this spy ring. Moltke, von Heumann and the Baroness. They are all obviously German. It would be essential, to my mind, that one of them should be able to pass himself off as a non-German, preferably an Englishman. I believe that Fuchs can do that. Perhaps he *is* an Englishman. I am sure that one of Fuchs' tasks is to get old Fisher to spill the beans about these new plans he has been drawing up for naval defences.'

'Shouldn't we warn Fisher then?'

'And let Fuchs know that we are on to him and his gang? No, but we must keep our eyes peeled.'

I nodded.

'Well, if you are going to be suspicious of Reggie Tew, then I'm laying odds on Doctor Fyson.'

Raffles looked interested.

'Why Fyson, Bunny?'

'Fyson is a German-speaker and Lord Toby said he was chairman of the Anglo-German League.'

'That seems a bit obvious. A spy would be a bit less conspicuous.'

'Well Fyson is unfriendly and stand offish,' I pointed out. 'I tried to speak to him earlier and the fellow was positively rude.'

'That doesn't make him a spy.'

'No, but it does make him suspicious.'

'Well, speaking of suspects what about this servant Cartwright,' Raffles pointed out.

I had nearly forgotten Cartwright.

'Did you learn anything more about him?' I asked.

Raffles shook his head.

'No, but he is certainly behaving in an odd manner. What better disguise could Fuchs have than that of a servant – the perfect position for eavesdropping.'

I agreed.

'Maybe Cartwright is our man.'

'Well,' sighed Raffles. 'I'm for bed. There's nothing we can do tonight. You wander around tomorrow and keep your eyes and ears open. We'd better make a check on the times of trains from London to see when von Heumann might arrive.'

'I'd nearly forgotten about him,' I said.

'Well, we will deal with him when the time comes,' replied Raffles.

The next morning after breakfast Raffles and the Baroness, properly accoutred, went off for their ride. I ate a more leisurely breakfast and decided that it was my task to keep an eye on Admiral Fisher. I reasoned that Fuchs would naturally gravitate towards the company of the Admiral and seek to engage him in conversation about naval matters.

I noticed that the admiral's breakfast was served by Cartwright who further engaged my suspicions by making a few elementary mistakes in the way he served the meal, such as serving from the left hand side of the guest until a sharp word from Tomkins, the butler, put the man right. It was obvious that Cartwright had not been in his present profession for very long.

My mind leapt from Cartwright to Fyson. After breakfast I observed that the Doctor insisted on going for a stroll with the admiral, much against the latter's will, though the doctor turned aside the admiral's protests in a bland manner. At that moment I would have placed my money on Fyson as our elusive Mr Fuchs. Then another idea formed in my mind. Perhaps Fyson and Cartwright were working together. While everyone engaged themselves in their strenuous morning pursuits, I resolved to make a brief search of Fyson's room. That would please Raffles.

I stood up and was about to leave the breakfast table when Reggie Tew came in.

'Lo, Manders!' he almost shrilled. 'want a word with you, you being a scribbler and all that. Wanted to discuss . . .'

I interrupted him pointedly and excused myself saying

that I had to meet Augusta Pellinore-Crudgett who, thankfully, had already breakfasted and departed for the village to visit the old Saxon Church for which it is renowned.

I hurriedly made my way to the guest room and bumped into a young maid who was packing dirty linen into a laundry basket.

'Er, do you know which is Doctor Fyson's room?' I asked, trying to sound casual. 'I promised to pick up a book and I forgot which room he told me it was.'

The young girl bobbed a curtsey and pointed down the corridor.

'Second door on the right, sir.'

The door was not locked. I breathed a small prayer of thanks. I entered and made a rapid inspection. On the dressing table was a small writing box, the sort one travels with. I opened it and glanced through the contents. There were numerous sheets of writing paper with a gothic letter heading announcing the Anglo-German League with an address in Highgate. There were some letters written in German and English but seemingly inocuous in content. At the bottom of the box were two photographs, individually framed in silver. One was of an elderly man and the other of a woman. On the back frame of the man's photograph was a legend: 'My father, Josiah Fyson'. On the back frame of the woman's photograph was a similar legend: 'Mein Mutter, Helga von Schasburg'.

I gasped with excitement.

Fyson was part German! He must be Fuchs!

'Did you find the book sir?'

The door had opened and the young maid stood looking at me.

I forced a smile, in spite of the blood rushing to my cheeks.

'No. That's odd. I thought he might have left it in here. I'll go down and speak to Doctor Fyson. Perhaps he has taken the book with him.'

The maid said nothing but set about her task of changing the bed linen.

I went downstairs to the library feeling a little shaky and praying the maid would not mention the incident to Fyson.

Lord Toby was in the study reading *The Times*.

'Toby,' I said, throwing myself into a leather covered armchair, 'how long have you known Fyson?'

Toby raised his eyes from his newspaper.

'Seward Fyson. About ten years or so. Why?'

'Where did you meet him?'

'Berlin, I think. Why?'

'I was just wondering what his interest in Germany was. You said he was chairman of the Anglo-German League and all that.'

'Fyson is mad keen on German literature. He's quite an expert on it, so I gather. Bilingual, you know. He is half-German himself. His mother was one of the von Schasburgs of Westphalia; a very well connected family.'

'Oh.'

I was rather disappointed. Had Fyson been hiding his German parentage it would have fitted my idea perfectly and made him a very suitable candidate for Fuchs. Anyway, I reasoned, that did not eliminate him from suspicion.

'Actually,' Lord Toby was saying, 'the fellow's asked me to give a talk next month to a meeting of his dashed league. Simply won't take a *no* for an answer. Just because I've been in the diplomatic service in Germany for a while.'

Tomkins came in with mid-morning coffee.

'Are you all set for the fancy dress ball, this evening?' asked Lord Toby, helping himself to a cup.

I nodded absently.

'Have you and your friend Roberts brought costumes.'

'Yes.'

'And masks? It's going to be a masked affair, you know.'

'I didn't forget,' I assured him.

'Excellent. I've hired a quartet from the Grand Hotel at Brighton to come up and play for us. It should be . . .'

Tomkins re-entered and coughed politely.

'Yes, Tomkins.'

'Your other guest has now arrived, sir. Colonel von Heumann.'

CHAPTER SIXTEEN

It was sheer luck that Raffles and I managed to avoid Oberst von Heumann all that Saturday.

Raffles and the Baroness had taken a picnic luncheon and were not due to return until the afternoon. As for myself, as soon as I heard Tomkins announce the arrival of von Heumann I made a bee-line for the village to have a word with the redoubtable Mister Cleophane of Dundee. On the way there I passed the Pellinore-Crudgetts' returning from their inspection of the Saxon Church. Lady Pellinore-Crudgett favoured me with a distant nod while Augusta giggled and added, for good measure, an 'Oh, I say!' Mister Cleophane of Dundee was sitting in the same position I had seen him in on the previous day.

'I've come to join you for luncheon, Mackenzie,' I said, dropping into the seat beside him.

He scowled.

'Are ye no supposed to be on the job?'

'It's my belief that we've solved the mystery,' I returned airily.

Mackenzie's eyes narrowed.

'Have ye now, laddie?' he breathed. 'Ye ken where the letters are then?'

'Not exactly,' I admitted. 'But I would start by having your men investigate the background of a Doctor Seward Fyson.'

Mackenzie noted the name down in a small black book and went off to make a telephone call to New Scotland Yard. He returned after a while with the landlord who bore two plates of hot cottage-pie and peas and two pints of ale.

Mackenzie peered at me.

'So ye reckon that this man Fyson is this mysterious Fuchs character?'

'That's my guess.'

'What does Mister Raffles say?'

I felt rather offended.

'I'm sure he'll agree with me when I tell him my suspicions,' I said off-handedly.

Mackenzie pursed his lips.

'Oh aye?'

There was something in his tone which I did not like.

'Anyway,' I said, 'von Heumann has arrived so I am keeping out of the way for a bit.'

'Ye'll have to meet yon fellow sooner or later,' observed Mackenzie.

I thought about matters for a while and then smiled.

'If Raffles and I can get back to our rooms without meeting the dratted fellow, we might be able to put that meeting off until tomorrow.'

'What? Stay in your rooms, you mean?'

'No. There's a masked fancy dress party tonight at the hall.'

'It's a chance, aye,' nodded Mackenzie.

I spent a less than pleasant two hours with the Chief Superintendent who insisted on turning the conversation to old times and trying to clear up some of the mysteries as to how Raffles and I had managed to elude him for so long. It was a topic of conversation that I was not particularly fond of pursuing.

At last I took off on a circuitous route back to the hall, hoping to intercept Raffles on the way. I prayed that we might elude von Heumann long enough to gain the relative safety of our rooms. After all, in that rather disastrous affair on the *Uhlan* it had been me whom von Heumann had identified at the subsequent trial and his evidence had caused me to serve my first and only term of imprisonment. It was obvious that I had not changed much during the intervening seven years or so.

With sinking heart, having had no sign of Raffles, I neared Hurstdevenish and was making my way across the lawns when a familiar voice hailed me.

'What joy, Bunny!'

Raffles, still in riding togs, was just crossing the lawn from the direction of the stables.

'Von Heumann is here!' I hissed, glancing round lest we be spotted.

Raffles' face darkened.

'Has he seen you?'

'No, I've been down at the village with Mackenzie.'

'Let's get back to our rooms,' suggested Raffles, and I made no demur.

Whoever is the god of luck, that individual was with us that day. We encountered no one on the journey to our rooms except Mrs Walker in the company of the majestic figure of Madam Doubrovska. We exchanged a brief pleasantry and then were safely in Raffles' room. Once there Raffles flung himself full-length on the bed and groaned.

'God, Bunny, I should have kept up my horse riding. I'm as stiff as a board. Help me off with my boots, old fellow.'

As I did so I quickly related my suspicions about Fyson.

'So you believe that the good doctor is Fuchs?' drawled Raffles when I had finished.

'All the evidence points to it.'

'Rather circumstantial,' he said lightly. 'Barely enough evidence to hang a dog.'

I was annoyed.

'Well, what information were you able to wrest from the Baroness?' I said not able to keep the sneer from my voice.

He shrugged.

'Not much at the moment but something will turn up shortly. I'm sure of it.'

He went into his washroom.

'Well, I suggest we stay here until this charade thing this evening,' I said. 'Once we can mingle with everyone in costume and masks there will be little chance of being recognised.'

Raffles nodded and pulled out his pocket watch.

'Five o'clock. What about some tea?'

I confess, I was thinking about the inner man at that moment.

'Just ring for the maid, old top,' called Raffles, above the running water. 'I'm for a bath. Just tell whoever comes we'd like tea here because we are too exhausted to join the others.'

I tugged at the bell rope.

After a while it was Cartwright who answered and took his instructions from me in a rather surly fashion.

'If Fyson is your man,' Raffles said, after he had gone, 'what about Cartwright then? He's a queer bird.'

'I think Cartwright is merely one of Fyson's men,' I said, airing my theory.

'My, my, Bunny. Your grey matter has been hard at work today,' Raffles replied lightly.

He disappeared to have his bath.

It was seven o'clock when Raffles and I went down to the dining room clad in our costumes. I had purchased a Harlequin outfit from a theatrical costumier in Orange Street which had a black mask that covered the entire top of the head. Raffles was clad in the costume of an Arabian sheik with wreaths of cloth around his face, which, with his mask, would have made it impossible for his own mother to recognise him.

The dining room had been cleared and trestle tables set alongside the walls on which food and drinks were laid out in buffet fashion. The great sliding wooden doors which partitioned the dining room from the ballroom had been pushed back and, on a small platform, a string quartet was valiantly scraping out popular dance tunes.

Lord Toby hurried to and fro organising, dressed in a cavalier costume and, although masked, was recognisable at a glance. So was Lord Fisher, skulking in a pirate costume, while the rest of the guests were clad in a variety of weird and exotic guises.

'Ah, there you fellows are,' boomed Lord Toby coming up to us. He hesitated and peered forward. 'It is you, isn't it?' Then he grinned. 'Well, can't be anyone else, can it?

Had me worried when you didn't turn up for tea. Arduous day, what? Never mind. Tomkins said you were both resting.'

He turned and waved to a tall, awkward looking cossack.

'You haven't met Colonel von Heumann, have you? Just arrived today'

The cossack bowed and we bowed back.

'This is Mister Roberts and my brother-in-law, Harry.'

The names meant nothing to the German who again clicked his heels and then gravitated towards an Indian Chieftain who was talking about his experiences exploring German South West Africa with the voice of Captain Walker.

A woman dressed in a Restoration costume with the most daring neckline that I have ever seen came up and laid her hand on Raffles. Her voice, deep and rich, was immediately recognisable as Baroness von Stalhein's.

'I missed you at tea,' there was a gentle rebuke in her voice. 'I did not know you were so tired by our ride.'

Raffles cleared his throat. His voice was husky.

'I was busy, actually. I had to catch up on some business papers.'

'I thought it was the custom in England that everything stopped for the English tea?'

With a laugh, Raffles drew her onto the dance floor.

I helped myself to a glass of champagne and looked around me. The Cossack was now engaged with a burly kilted Scots chieftain who, under his mask, sported Fyson's beard. I smiled in satisfaction. Everything Fyson did confirmed my suspicion of him.

An arm caught mine.

'I know it is forward of me, Mister Manders,' said Mrs Walker's breathless voice, 'but I shall die if I do not have a dance. My husband is quite neglectful of me.'

She was clad in some sort of middle-European peasant costume, with a low cut white blouse and full sleeves, a tight black bodice and a full but fairly short skirt.

I put down my glass and offered her my arm.

She was a marvellous dancer, much better than poor

Alice. We danced not one dance but several. She danced with an easy intimacy, her warm body close against mine, and several times I glanced towards the Indian Chieftain in apprehension. He seemed too deep in conversation to spare a look in our direction.

'I could do with a glass of champagne now, Mister Manders,' smiled Mrs Walker, pushing her way off the floor. 'La, but it's hot in here. Will you bring it to me on the terrace?'

I did as she bade me and followed her through the french windows.

She was sitting on the marble balustrade staring into the night when I brought the champagne to her.

'You are an excellent dancer . . . Harry,' she said, after sipping slowly at the champagne. 'I may call you Harry, mayn't I?'

I said she may, adding that I was a mere amateur dancer compared with her.

'I do so love dancing,' she said rather wistfully. 'The trouble with Harold, that is Captain Walker, is that he hates dancing.'

'What a shame,' I murmured sympathetically.

'Isn't it?' she agreed. 'But you like dancing, don't you, Harry?'

I said I did for I felt it was expected of me. To be truthful, I always felt somewhat of a fool gyrating over a dance floor.

'Would you think it terribly forward of me, if I made a suggestion?'

I frowned.

'Next weekend Harold, that is Captain Walker, is off to Africa for six months,' she continued in a breathless rush. 'You know, it is something to do with this corporation Lord Toby is organising. Well, he's off to organise it in some ghastly place – Alexander Bay, I think, somewhere down in southern Africa. I couldn't bear to go with him. But life in London can be pretty lonely and dreary. Would you think it forward of me if I asked you to call on me after Harold, that is Captain Walker has gone? I would love to go dancing some time.'

I stared at her in some surprise, blushing deeply.

'I . . . er, I am married,' I ventured.

'Silly boy,' returned Mrs Walker. 'So am I. That has nothing to do with it.'

I tried to conjure up a mental picture of Alice but somehow it failed to stay formed for very long.

'I er I'd be delighted to call,' I said huskily.

'Oh *splendid*!' she exclaimed in delight. Then, before I realised it, she had leaned forward and fastened herself to me in a passionate embrace, her mouth hungrily against mine. She drew away, a trifle breathlessly, her eyes dancing.

'We can't talk here,' she whispered conspiratorially. 'My husband might spot us. Do you know where our room is – second floor, east wing, third door along on the right of the corridor. Join me there in fifteen minutes.'

I opened my mouth to object but she leant forward and silenced me with a soft, quick kiss upon the lips.

'Fifteen minutes,' she hissed and was gone.

I stood there gaping and wondering what I had let myself in for. What would Alice say? No, that did not dare thinking about.

The sound of someone clearing their throat made me glance up blushing in guilt.

Raffles stood leaning against the french window in his Arab costume.

'Well now, Bunny,' he said softly. 'I would never have thought you were a gad-about, and with a married lady too. What would Alice say?'

Was there a hint of mimicry in his voice as he aired my thought of a moment before?

'Dash it all, Raffles,' I cried hotly, 'the woman damned near ravished me! It was nothing to do with me!'

'Hush!' snapped Raffles. 'You clot, do you want everyone to hear? I declare that you are being rather caddish about the affair. Poor Mrs Walker – her name is Clarissa, by the by. She has quite a reputation as a man-eater. Are you taking up her invitation to go dancing?'

'Of course not,' I returned shortly.

'You could do worse, old chap. She is quite a good looker.'

'I happened to be happily married.'

'I don't see what that has to do with it,' murmured Raffles.

'You can be a bit of a bounder at times,' I snorted.

Raffles chuckled.

'Realistic is the word I think you mean, Bunny. Anyway, I didn't come out here to natter about your *affaires de coeur*. I've noticed that our friend Cartwright has been taking a lively interest in hovering around old Admiral Fisher. Thought you ought to know.'

He nodded and turned back into the ballroom.

I looked at my watch a little guiltily and then turned angrily for the ballroom. Before I had gone one step I halted. Dash it all! I had promised the woman I would join her in fifteen minutes. It would be frightfully caddish of me not to. I was a gentleman, after all. Yes, I'd go and see her and explain that it would be morally wrong of me, being married, and her, being married, to meet up in London and go dancing together. Yes, that was it. I'd go and explain.

I turned and made my way to the second floor of the east wing. I paused before the third door on the right and knocked lightly.

'Who is it?' came Clarissa Walker's voice, that soft breathless voice.

'Me,' I said. 'Harry Manders.'

I heard a rustling sound. Then: 'It's open, Harry. Come in and close the door behind you.'

I entered. The room was in total darkness.

'I say . . .' I began.

'Close the door and put the latch on.'

Unthinkingly, I did so.

'Hang it,' I muttered, 'I can't see you.'

'I'm over here on the bed.'

I started in the direction of the voice, hands outstretched.

'Lor', Clarissa,' I said, 'have the lights fused or something . . .?'

A giggle answered me and a cold hand reached forward to mine and drew me onto the bed. The dark form of Clarissa Walker was lying there. Her hand, still encircling my wrist, guided my hand to her face. I felt her soft warm lips brush against my palm. Then she had guided my hand to the smooth roundness of her shoulder and across to her . . .

Dash it all! The woman was lying there stark naked.

Now I'm a gentleman but I do happen to be a man: after all, it would have been rather insulting to have left her in that condition then and there. Well, I ask you, what would you have done in the circumstances? My old Games Master used to say that rules are made for the obedience of fools and the guidance of wise men. Well, Harry Manders was no fool and Clarissa Walker provided all the guidance I needed.

An hour passed and I did not think of Alice once.

Finally, Clarissa sat up and started to hunt for her clothes.

'I'd better go back downstairs before Harold misses me,' she said, pulling on her peasant costume over her exquisite body.

I agreed.

'Won't he have missed you already?' I asked, worried by the passage of time.

'Not yet,' she shrugged. 'He can talk about his beastly African explorations for hours at a time whether anyone is listening or not.'

I scrambled back into my costume while she straightened the bed.

'I think I'll turn in now, anyway,' I said, checking my wristwatch.

Clarissa opened the door and then smiled coquettishly at me.

'Until next weekend in London then?'

I kissed her softly on the lips and nodded.

Dash it, what is a chap expected to do in the circumstances?

I made my way to the main staircase and up to the third floor, turning into the corridor where Raffles and I had our rooms. I was still thinking about the delights of making love to Clarissa Walker when a noise caused me to halt in mid-stride. I peered cautiously into the corridor.

It was shrouded in gloom but I saw something which brought my heart into my mouth. There, crouching down by the lock of the door of Raffles' room, was a dark figure, obviously trying to gain entrance by forcing the lock.

CHAPTER SEVENTEEN

I have remarked before that I am not by any means a bold person.

When I saw the dark shadow of a man hovering in the corridor outside Raffles' room, my heart leapt into my throat. For a moment I resolved to retrace my steps back down the stairway and rejoin my fellow guests whose laughter and merry-making still echoed from the floors below.

Then I rebuked myself firmly. After all, what would Raffles do in this situation?

He was somewhere below trying to elicit information from the beautiful Baroness von Stalhein and so, it would appear, while he was thus engaged one of the Baroness's confederates was about to search his room. I had a duty and an allegiance to Raffles.

Taking my courage in both hands I stepped into the corridor and demanded in a voice which used volume to disguise its tremulous note: 'What do you think you're doing, my man?'

Before I knew what had hit me, the shadow bending before the lock of the door had turned with a smothered exclamation, had leapt past me, pushing me so hard against the wall that for a moment I was completely stunned and slumped there gasping for breath.

I do not know what came into my head because the

following instant, on recovering, I was pursuing the figure down the corridor. Perhaps it was natural anger at being ill-used that spurred me to the pursuit. The figure ran wildly, nearly colliding several times with vases and other decorative items with which Lord Toby's country residence was generously filled.

'Hey!' I yelled as I ran. 'Stop . . . stop there!'

I followed the figure through a maze of corridors until we appeared to enter the servants' quarters at the back of the house whence my quarry fled down a small staircase. There, for a moment, I lost sight of him and paused by the bannister rail to regain my breath.

Then the sound of a stumbling footfall down the stairway made me plunge on again.

Was it Fuchs that I was pursuing? The thought momentarily crossed my mind and made me shiver in apprehension.

Nevertheless, I pressed on. The stairway ran down into what was obviously the main servants' hall, devoid of servants now as they were in attendance at the party in the main part of the house.

Here I hesitated a fraction wondering which way to go.

The slamming of a door from a room further on told me.

I was away like a hound, wishing that Raffles could be there to see that at times I, too, could display dogged determination and pluck.

I came into a smaller room, obviously a pantry used by the maids, but which had a pair of french windows opening onto the midnight blackened lawn which surrounded the house. They were open, with a faint night breeze catching at the muslin of the curtains.

Without a second's hesitation, fortified by my elation at my new found courage, I hurried through the windows and stood looking around the shadowed lawn.

There was little to see. Everything was in darkness.

Abruptly there came the sound of a sharp *crack*! as if someone had broken a stick.

The sound had a familiarity and, with my stomach

turning somersaults within me, I realised that I had heard the report of a pistol.

I stood waiting on the lawn, fully expecting the noise to raise the household and for a commotion to break out. But there was nothing but silence, unless one counted the distant sound of dance music from the front of the house.

After a short while, when I realised that the houseparty had not heard the sound, probably because the noise of the party had drowned the report of the firearm, there came to me the cold realisation that I alone was a witness to the shot. Even the servants, engaged in their various pursuits, would probably not have heard the noise or, if they had, were not of the inquisitive type.

My blood was chilled as an awful thought went through me.

What if the man I had been pursuing had found Raffles and shot him?

I simply had to find out what had happened. The report of the firearm had come from the direction of the darkened summer house which stood in the middle of the lawn some hundred yards away.

I squared my shoulders and marched slowly forward, my feet making no sound on the dew sodden grass.

The summer house was in total blackness and I wished that I had not left my pocket torch in my suit, but the torch would have been bulky to carry around in my Harlequin outfit.

The door was half open when I reached it and I gave it a cautious shove.

As I did so the moon broke out from behind a cloud bank and shone a beam of light into the place.

The dark figure of a man was leaning against the furthest wall, his back was half turned towards me.

'Wh . . . who are you?' I said, trying to sound commanding but only succeeding in sounding querulous.

There was no answer.

Some storm clouds chased each other across the white face of the moon and the summer house was plunged in blackness again. I suddenly remembered my matches and these I took from my pocket and advanced towards the figure.

'Who's there?' I demanded again, this time reaching out a hand to touch the man's shoulder.

I almost screamed as the form before me collapsed in a heap on the floor. My hand felt wet and sticky where I had touched the man and in the flickering light of my matches I saw that it was stained red.

It was a battle to quieten my panicking thoughts and I tried to keep the concern for Raffles' welfare fixed firmly in my mind.

Slowly I bent down and examined the dead man.

He was dressed in a cossack's costume.

'My God!' I gasped involuntarily, removing the mask and looking on the perpendicular moustaches with their waxed spires. 'Oberst von Heumann!'

It was indeed the officious little German. He had been shot in the chest. Blood had splattered across the front of his cossack jacket. His eyes were glazed and staring.

A groan from a corner of the summer house made the hair prick on the nape of my neck.

I turned to flee, my teeth grinding against each other to stop them chattering.

The groan came again. It was the groan of a man in pain.

I raised my match and peered into the dark corner.

A second man was lying on his back on the floor.

I moved beside him.

The flickering flame of my match revealed the contorted features of the suspicious footman, Cartwright. There was no reason to ask why he was in pain. The handle of a long bone carving knife, the type that is usually used for carving meat, was protruding from his chest.

He groaned again and his eyes tried to focus on me.

'Is that . . . is that Manders?'

His breath was coming in wheezy grunts.

'Yes,' I affirmed. 'I am Harry Manders.'

'You . . . you must tell them . . . tell them . . . the fox

. . . the fox will pass them on. Monday morning. Rotten Row. The fox is . . . fox is . . .'

A sudden spasm shook his body. He gave a long quivering sigh and was silent.

The cold sweat stood out on my forehead.

Fighting down an overpowering impulse to run, I managed to walk calmly from the summer house, closing the door behind me. Slowly, I retraced my steps back to my room and washed the blood marks from my hands, observing carefully to see whether any blood had splattered on my suit. It was an effort to do this carefully and calmly. My instinct was to immediately go in seach of Raffles or to find a telephone and ring Mackenzie. But I forced myself to remain calm. After all, Raffles would do as much.

Having washed up and swallowed two well filled glasses of malt whisky from my traveller's flask, I went slowly downstairs to rejoin the party.

Clarissa Walker gave me a little wave as I entered the ballroom. She was standing dutifully by her husband as he continued to drone forth about his African experiences. I forced myself to smile in her direction.

I found Raffles still in animated conversation with the Baroness who was sitting back with a contented smile upon her face. Somehow I caught his eyes and by elaborate pantomime managed to convince him that I had to speak with him urgently.

In a moment he joined me on the terrace.

'What the devil is it, Bunny?' he said, a little aggressively. I gathered he was unhappy at my interrupting his tête-a-tête with the Baroness.

Without preamble, I blabbed my news.

Raffles gave a long, low whistle.

'This is deuced awkward, Bunny.'

I thought that was an understatement.

'What shall we do?' I asked, somewhat agitated. 'There'll be a frightful stink when the bodies are discovered.'

'There certainly will,' he agreed. 'But what's more to the point is the apparent fact that Cartwright was obviously working for our side and was not a German agent at all, as you suspected.'

I scratched my ear.

'What did he mean about the fox?'

Raffles gazed at me in annoyance.

'My dear Bunny,' he said heavily, 'the fox is but a literal translation of Fuchs. Fuchs is going to hand the letters over to the courier on Monday morning in Rotten Row. The courier will then take them out of the country. Damn it, and the man was just about to tell you who Fuchs was when he died.'

He paused and pursed his lips.

'I wonder how the poor fellow found out?'

'Well, he paid for doing so,' I observed.

'That's true,' replied Raffles. 'From what you say, it seems that von Heumann was onto him, discovered him and stabbed him. Then Cartwright shot von Heumann in self defence.'

A curious look crossed Raffles' face.

'But strange that, though. I wouldn't have thought von Heumann would resort to stabbing a fellow with a meat cleaver. After all, he's an officer and all that. They have a particularly strong code of military ethics at Heidelberg. It just doesn't seem the sort of thing a fellow from a noble *junker* family would do, does it?'

'Well, that's how it appeared to me,' I said defensively.

'I'm sure you're right, Bunny,' he replied, gripping my shoulder. 'You've done well. But it is going to be deucedly awkward if the bodies of Cartwright and von Heumann are discovered before Monday morning.'

'Why?'

'Because now we know exactly where and when Fuchs is handing over the letters, and can lay a trap for him, we don't want to do anything that will scare him off. I think it better if we can arrange to have them hidden for the next two days.'

He turned and was leading the way round the house towards the summer house.

'How can we do that, Raffles?' I gasped, falling into step with him.

I could see him grinning in the gloom.

'Why, our dear old friend Mackenzie of the Yard will have to help. We'll drag the bodies across the lawn to the woods. Then you can nip off smartish to the village and get Mackenzie . . .'

I groaned loudly. I was seeing far too much of the road to the village.

'. . . Mackenzie can arrange for his men to collect the bodies,' Raffles was continuing, 'and he can hush the whole thing up for a day or two.'

Raffles came to a halt at the door of the summer house.

'Are they in here?' he asked quietly.

I grunted in affirmation.

He opened the door and peered in, taking from the folds of his voluminous Arab costume the small pocket torch which rarely fails to accompany him.

He was silent for a moment and then drew back with a frown.

'What is it?' I asked anxiously looking at his bewildered face.

He made no reply but handed me the torch and motioned me to look inside.

I did so, with some reluctance.

My jaw dropped in astonishment.

There was no sign of the bodies of Oberst von Heumann nor of the servant Cartwright.

They had vanished.

CHAPTER EIGHTEEN

After a long silence, Raffles turned to me. I could not see his face but could feel the question in his eyes.

'They *were* here,' I said desperately.

'I'm sure they were, if you say so,' replied Raffles. 'The point is, what has happened to them?'

I shrugged helplessly.

'Fuchs must have been here before us,' declared Raffles

emphatically. 'How long has it been since you left the bodies?'

'No more than ten minutes.'

'Fuchs must have some confederates nearby.'

I peered around and shivered slightly.

'Look, Bunny, you'd best fling a coat over that ghastly costume of yours and nip down to the White Bull and raise Mackenzie. Tell him everything that has happened but, in heaven's name, don't tell him about Rotten Row or he'll have the place swarming with policemen and ruin the whole game . . .'

'But will Fuchs go to Rotten Row now?'

'Yes; unless he thinks we know about Cartwright and von Heumann. Did anyone see you discover the bodies?'

I shook my head.

'Not that I know of.'

'Then we must work on the assumption that Fuchs believes that no one else knows that Cartwright and von Heumann killed each other. We'll let him think that he's covered his tracks. That's why it's important not to let Mackenzie know too much. Cartwright must have been one of his men, so Mackenzie's been playing a double game with us. Given a chance, Mackenzie could blow the whole gaff, to use a peterman's parlance.'

I sighed: I was getting really annoyed about my trips to the White Bull and it was after one o'clock in the morning.

'What'll you do?'

'I'll get back to the party and see if I can find out what has happened to von Heumann . . .'

'But we *know*,' I was puzzled.

'I mean, find out what excuse is being made for his sudden disappearance,' explained Raffles patiently. 'Fuchs will have to make some excuse for von Heumann's disappearance and that may well bring him into the open.'

We left the deserted summer house and made our way back to the house. A french window was open leading into the hall and I told Raffles that I would get my coat and find Mackenzie. Raffles nodded and went towards the ballroom. Just as he passed from my range of vision I heard the obnoxious treble of Reggie Tew greet him.

'Out for a smoke, old boy? Good idea, what?'

Raffles made some sort of reply and I thought I heard a second voice join the conversation. I did not pay any further heed but hurried to my room, seized my coat and was away down to the village.

It was lucky for me that Mackenzie had told me which room he was staying in. I had to resort to the handful of gravel technique, and had to throw several handfuls against the window before Mackenzie's irate tones came down to me. As soon as I identified myself, his head vanished and a few moments later he joined me in the porch of the old inn. As briefly as I could, omitting on Raffles' instructions what Cartwright had said about the rendezvous point, I told Mackenzie what had happened. His face grew longer and his eyes went wide.

'Good God! Cartwright dead, ye say?'

I nodded.

'Poor fellow. He was one o' my men from Special Branch.'

'Raffles thought as much. What was he doing at Hurstdevenish?'

Mackenzie looked uncomfortable.

'When you told me about the weekend party and that Fuchs was going to be there, I arranged for Cartwright to go down as a servant. I thought an extra man on the spot would help and maybe provide some leads.'

'Well,' I said, 'the poor boob stuck out like a sore thumb. You could see he wasn't a servant. We thought, at first, he was Fuchs or one of his henchmen.'

Mackenzie said nothing.

'Well, Raffles told me to tell you what happened and I have. I'll be off back to the hall now.'

'Is this cricket match between the guests at the hall and the villagers still scheduled for tomorrow?' the Chief Superintendent asked moodily.

'As far as I know,' I replied.

'Then I'll see you at the match. Keep me informed if anything else occurs.'

I raised my hand and trudged back to the hall again. The party seemed to be breaking up when I reached there. No one apparently had noticed my absence. I had a final drink and went to my room.

It was not long afterwards that I thought I heard Raffles and the Baroness pass down the corridor towards her room. I sat up expecting him to return and ask for a report of what Mackenzie had said. However, I was not really surprised when he did not, nor did I hear him pass by to his own room. I finally turned off the light and closed my eyes.

I had only just fallen asleep when I was roused by the sharp click of the door.

Someone had entered my room.

'That you, Raffles?' I asked groggily and switched on the bedside light.

'Turn off the light, please.'

Clarissa Walker stood just inside the door. She was wrapped in a rather stunning and revealing négligée – a frilly loose gown which barely covered her long limbs.

I turned off the light, my mouth going dry.

'What are you doing here?' My voice came as a croak.

She gave a throaty chuckle and her dark figure came across to the bed. Before I realised what she was about she had slipped off her négligée and slipped between the sheets, her warm body pressing against mine, her mouth demanding on my lips.

'I say . . .' I gasped.

'Hush!' she commanded. 'It's all right. That pig Harold came to bed stone drunk and smelling like a brewery. He's in our room now snoring like the pig he is. Not even the announcement of Armageddon would wake him. He'll snore away until morning.'

Her cool hands started to fumble with my pyjama jacket.

'Steady on, Clarissa,' I mumbled. 'We really shouldn't be doing this . . .'

She bent her head and nibbled my ear.

'Can you think of anything better to do?'

I sighed and resigned myself to a sleepless night.

140

It was just before dawn that Clarissa let herself out of my room and slipped quietly back to her own. Then, and only then, was I able to close my eyes and sink off into a deep sleep.

Raffles awoke me pretty late.

'Stir yourself, Bunny,' he admonished. 'It's nearly ten o'clock.'

I glanced in surprise at my wristwatch and leapt out of bed. Raffles was leaning against the door jamb of the adjoining door to his room and smiling at me.

'You look as if you have had a rough night,' he murmured.

I shot him a suspicious look. He was immaculately dressed in his cricket whites, not a hair out of place and looked fresh and well-rested. He pulled out his cigarette case and lit up a Sullivan.

'Did you learn anything further while I was with Mackenzie?' I called, running the water for a quick bath.

Raffles exhaled.

'I casually asked the Baroness's brother, the young aide to the ambassador, where his colleague had disappeared to. The young chap said that he heard that he had been recalled to London and had gone off in the embassy car. I had to cleverly box to get more details. The story was that a telephone call had come through from the embassy and one of the servants had asked von Heumann to take it. Naturally, the servant was said to have been Cartwright. Trouble was, I could not find out where the story emanated from. Of course, no one actually saw von Heumann leave.'

'I heard Reggie Tew spot you when you returned from the summer house,' I commented, splashing myself in the bath.

Raffles shrugged.

'He, Lord Toby and Fyson were smoking on the terrace. I'd said I'd just gone for a walk and a smoke. What did Mackenzie say about Cartwright?'

'He admitted that Cartwright was one of his men – a Special Branch officer. Hand me that towel, Raffles.'

Raffles stubbed out his cigarette and threw me the bath towel.

'Poor boob!' he muttered.

'That's what I told Mackenzie,' I said, vigorously towelling myself.

'It would seem that Mackenzie doesn't trust us.'

'I don't suppose you can blame him after all these years,' I pointed out.

'Well, we'll have to start playing the ball close to the chest. As soon as this match is over we'll catch the train to London and be ready in Rotten Row at about six o'clock on Monday morning.'

I frowned as I pulled on my cricket flannels.

'Why so early?'

'Cartwright didn't specify what time in the morning that Fuchs was to meet his courier there, did he? He simply said *morning*, and that could mean anytime from midnight onwards. But, using logic, I think the time Fuchs would choose would be when there are several people about, maybe sometime between eight o'clock and ten o'clock. You know, the time when people in Park Lane go up for their morning constitutionals. But it will be best if we are in position as early as possible. Cheer up, Bunny. By midday on Monday we should have this beastly mess sorted out.'

He yawned and pulled out his pocket watch.

'Good Lor', we'd better get down to brekker.'

It was about ten-thirty when we went into the breakfast room. Only Lord Toby was sitting there with Madam Doubrovska. Tomkins greeted me with a plate of my favourite devilled kidneys and a pile of bacon. Raffles chose fruit juice and dry toast.

'Where's your new man – Cartwright?' I asked casually of Lord Toby.

Raffles shot me a murderous glance which made me turn red.

Lord Toby was frowning.

'Cartwright? The agency man? Oh, he's gone. He was only hired until last night to help out at the party. Why do you ask?'

I thought furiously, trying to save the situation.

'Oh, you remember that I told you that I thought I had seen him somewhere before. I thought it might have been at Lady Ridley's house. I was going to ask him if he'd been about.'

This seemed to satisfy Lord Toby because he grunted and returned to his breakfast.

Raffles caught my eye with a baleful glance. I grimaced. I thought I'd carried off the whole thing rather well. At least we had established that no one was at all suspicious of the disappearance of von Heumann or Cartwright. Fuchs was covering himself well.

I suddenly realised that Madam Doubrovska was talking to me.

'So you know the so elegant Lady Ridley?'

I hastily swallowed a mouthful of kidneys.

'I have that honour.'

'She is so charming,' went on Madam Doubrovska. 'So charming, a great patroness of the dance.'

She fixed me with her eyes.

'We have not talked much, Mister Manders. You have told me that you are interested in the dance.'

I smiled.

'Purely in an amateur fashion,' I said.

'Ah, amateur – for the love of the art. That is the meaning, is it not. That is how all art should be approached. Amateur. It comes from the Latin *amator* – a lover, does it not?'

I supposed it did.

'Ah, what an expressive language is your English,' went on the woman rolling her eyes. 'Do you not think so, Toby.'

She pronounced his name 'Too-bee'. Lord Toby coloured a little and said it probably was.

At that moment Captain Walker came in, his eyes were red and his hands unsteady. Doctor Fyson was with him. They helped themselves to coffee and ordered toast.

'Anyone seen Clarissa?' demanded Walker.

I could not stop my face from going bright red. I saw Raffles give me a pitying glance.

'Believe she's gone for a walk with Lady Pellinore-Crudgett and Augusta,' muttered Lord Toby.

Walker grunted, swallowed his coffee and left.

'A strange man, is that, Toby,' announced Madam Doubrovska. 'He was quite intoxicated last night.'

Lord Toby sighed.

'Yes, he is rather a heavy drinker, Anna.'

At that moment I happened to glance up and see that Fyson was looking at Raffles, who was finishing his breakfast. There was a strange look in his eye. That look renewed all my suspicions about Fyson. I was sure that he was Fuchs.

'Morning everyone.'

Admiral Fisher appeared at the french windows and stood surveying the breakfast table. The old sea-dog looked decidedly out of place in his cricket whites.

'Morning, admiral,' grunted Lord Toby. 'All set for the match then?'

The admiral nodded.

'All ready to make a century,' announced the First Sea Lord with satisfaction. 'Think these villagers are up to it, Devenish?'

Lord Toby smiled.

'They've a good eleven, Admiral.'

'Capital! Capital! I like a close run game.'

Lord Toby suddenly caught sight of the clock on the mantleshelf. He stood up.

'I'll have to hurry you, I'm afraid. We promised to start the match at eleven-thirty on the village green. By the time we walk down to the village . . .'

Everyone, it seemed, had the good sense to don their cricket whites before breakfasting so that we were all ready. Our team was to consist of Lord Toby, Lord Fisher, Captain Walker, Doctor Fyson, Sir Peter Lonsdale, Lord Bellamy, Jason Sickert, Lieutenant Symes, Reggie Tew, Raffles and myself.

The German ambassador, his aide, the ladies and other guests would come along to spectate and champion our side.

Tomkins, the butler, who was also going to be one of

our umpires for the game, organised a party of three servants in loading picnic hampers onto the pony and trap which would provide the midday meal.

We set out in procession following the pony and trap down to the village. I was a bit nervous when Clarissa Walker fell in step with me. I saw the captain giving her a disapproving stare but she seemed oblivious to it.

'A marvellous day for the match,' she said, motioning at the bright blue sky.

I nodded, silently.

'I hope you had a good rest last night,' she went on wickedly, rolling her eyes. 'You'll need your strength for your innings.'

I blushed crimson.

A little ahead Raffles was walking with the Baroness. She was holding onto his arm and glancing up at him every now and again with a look close to adoration on her exquisite features. Damn it! I wish I could feel as confident and at ease with women as he did.

CHAPTER NINETEEN

The late Sunday morning was hot and fine. There wasn't a cloud in the azure sky. Lord Toby shepherded us down to the village green, a rich green sward in front of the White Bull on which a white marquee had already been erected while, spread around the green turf, a crowd had gathered with rugs and picnic hampers. I spied Mackenzie almost at once, clad in rather garish plus-fours and a matching check jacket looking decidedly ill at ease, sitting by the tent. The crowd, mainly villagers, gave a ragged cheer as we appeared. A group of raw-boned giants, clad in cricket whites, stood outside the White Bull, several still had tankards in their hands.

A little man in clerical grey, with rabbit teeth, came forward and raised his hat to Lord Toby.

'Morning m'lord.'

'Morning, vicar,' returned Lord Toby, pumping the man's hand. I saw him wince under the grip.

'So, Prestwick,' went on Toby obliviously, 'are you umpiring today?'

The Reverend Prestwick nodded.

'If that is in order, your lordship.'

'Excellent. Excellent. Our umpire is Tomkins.'

Vicar and butler exchanged a handshake.

'Well, is everything ready?' asked Lord Toby, turning to us. We looked at each other. Eleven self-conscious men in cricket flannels. For myself I had no inclination whatsoever to take part in the match. I kept seeing the awful vision of Cartwright and von Heumann in the summer house. No sooner had I blotted that vision out than the seductive picture of Clarissa Walker began to cloud my thoughts. I had no heart for cricket. I cast a look at Raffles. He seemed oblivious to everything. He stood smiling broadly at the Baroness who was leaning towards him brushing some real or imaginery speck of dust from his shoulder. I had a deep suspicion that Raffles was getting serious about the woman. His apparent calm after the events of the previous night served to annoy me somewhat. I looked round. Everything seemed so unreal. The sleepy village, the cricket match, that lazy hot Sunday.

'Come on, chaps!' called Lord Toby. 'Are we all together?'

We gathered round Lord Toby, our self appointed captain, who introduced us to the village eleven with whom we solemnly shook hands. Meanwhile, Tomkins and the vicar had taken the stumps out and set them up. When this was done Reverend Prestwick returned, produced a coin and flicked it into the air – somewhat expertly, I considered. He gave an enquiring look at Lord Toby.

'Tails!' decided Lord Toby.

'Tails it is m'lord,' replied the vicar, scooping up the coin.

Lord Toby cleared his throat.

'Your team into bat first,' he told the village captain; a tall red-haired man named Larkin whose muscles rippled beneath his shirt as if he had but to breathe and the shirt would be rent asunder. I gathered that Larkin was the local smithy and he certainly grasped his bat as if it were a smith's hammer, wielding it like a dangerous weapon in his mighty fists.

Larkin and another man went into position while Lord Toby allocated his field, placing himself as wicket-keeper. Thankfully I found myself placed at long stop, a position which suited me down to the ground for few balls ever seemed to come my way. Raffles was asked to bowl the first over. To be truthful, I do not like cricket and if I had my choice I would never have played another beastly game after leaving school. Unfortunately my association with Raffles had forced me into one or two games in my time. Not that Raffles was a cricket fanatic, though his name and that of the game seemed inseparable in some people's minds.

Certainly as a cricketer he is without peer. He is a dangerous bat, a brilliant field and the very finest slow bowler of his decade. But at that it ended. To Raffles, cricket was merely a means to an end. He once told me:

'Cricket like everything else, is good enough sport until you discover a better. As a source of excitement it isn't in it with other things you wot of, Bunny, and the involuntary comparison becomes a bore. What's the satisfaction of taking a man's wicket when you want his spoons? Still, if you can bowl a bit your low cunning won't get rusty, and always looking for the weak spot's just the kind of mental exercise one wants. Yes, perhaps there's some affinity between the two things after all. But I'd chuck up cricket tomorrow, Bunny, if it wasn't for the glorious protection it affords a person of my proclivities.'

I recall remonstrating with him that cricket brought him before the public gaze in a way that was dangerous to his nocturnal profession.

'But, dear Bunny,' he had replied, 'that's exactly where you make a mistake. To follow crime with reasonable impunity you simply must have a parallel ostensible career – the more public the better. The principle is obvious. Mr Peace, of pious memory, disarmed suspicion by acquiring a local reputation for playing the fiddle and taming animals, and it's my profound conviction that Jack the Ripper was a really eminent public man, whose speeches were very likely reported alongside his atrocities. Fill the bill in some prominent part, and you'll never be suspected of doubling it with another of equal prominence. That's why I want you to cultivate journalism, my boy, and sign all you can. And it's the one and only reason why I don't burn my bats for firewood.'

'Manders!'

The agonised cry interrupted my reverie.

I glanced up startled just in time to see a high ball, smacked from Larkin's bat, curving down towards me. For a split second I stood in indecision, tried to lunge for it and missed it by a yard. A loud groan echoed round the field followed by some enthusiastic cheering from the villagers. Red with mortification I retrieved the ball from my feet and hurled it towards Raffles who was just finishing his second over.

Larkin had managed to score seven runs in that over, hitting a four and picking up three runs from my dropped catch. Captain Walker tried his luck next. I moved to my new position, hanging my head shamefully before my team-mates. Still, I never pretended to be a cricketer.

Larkin knocked up no less than three sixes from Walker's over and then Raffles went in to bowl again. I found myself watching him, trying to concentrate on the game. One did not have to be an expert at the game to appreciate his perfect command of pitch and break, his beautifully easy action which never varied with the varying pace . . . the infinite ingenuity of a versatile attack. It was no mere exhibition of athletic prowess, it was an intellectual treat, and one with a special significance in my eyes. I saw the 'affinity between the two things', saw it in that morning's tireless warfare. His bowling was a combination of resource and cunning, of patience and precision, of head-work and handiwork, which made every over an artistic whole.

Larkin, in opposition to Raffles, used his big broad frame and his strength as his weapons. He would strike out with great smashing strokes, more often than not hitting fours and sixes for bowlers other than Raffles. With Raffles he had to be content in merely blocking the ball and, eventually, in the fourth over he fell to Raffles' slow, deliberate precision.

Lunchtime arrived with a great deal of relief for me. The village side had decided to declare at eighty-six for seven and allow Lord Toby's eleven to go into bat immediately after luncheon. We were able to wash in the White Bull and sit down to cold meats, salads and beer in the marquee. I was not able to have a word with Raffles alone, he seemed to positively hog the Baroness's company and, much to my embarrassment, Clarissa Walker insisted on sitting by me and offering her sympathy about my dropped catch.

Lord Toby was a believer in putting in his weakest men to bat first: a reverse of the strategy employed by the village eleven who had put their strong men in and, after their defence crumbled, the demoralised weaker batsmen were soon put to flight. Lord Toby believed that putting his weakest men in first gave them a sense of determination against letting the side down and gave the stronger batsmen a better resolve when their turn came. So it was, with some small humiliation, that I was nominated first bat with Jason Sickert as second.

To my horror I found myself facing the red haired blacksmith, Larkin, who seemed to take a run three times as long as any other bowler that I have seen. By the time he reached the stumps, his legs were going like steam pistons, his arm went back and the ball – well, I never saw it. It was so fast. I felt something pass me to my off-stump and heard the smack of leather as the wicket-keeper scooped it up. It had just missed my stumps.

To my annoyance Larkin moved down the pitch to retrieve the ball and grinned nastily at me.

'Sorry, sir. I thought you were ready.'

I scowled back.

Back walked the beastly man to his point, then down he came again like an express train.

This time I judged where the ball might be, raised my

bat and felt it vibrate in my hands as the leather ball cannoned into it. The shock numbed my wrists and the ball bounced back a yard. The wicket-keeper went forward to recover it and gave me a pitying look.

I tried to summon my courage. I had survived two balls from the red haired giant. There was no need to suppose I could survive four more.

Down came Larkin again. I closed my eyes in expectation. Out went my bat. Thump!

'Run, Manders! Run, dammit!'

It was my fellow batsman, Jason Sickert, charging down the pitch.

I shook myself and ran.

I had made a single and felt extraordinarily pleased with myself.

My colleague met with the next ball and hit it for four. Then he scored a two and then blocked for the last ball of the over.

The second over was bowled by a slow bowler, a thick set man whom someone told me at luncheon was the local sexton. I was able to hit five runs from his more leisurely paced balls. Then, stupidly, I scored a single with the last ball of the over – stupidly because it meant that I had to face Larkin's bowling again.

I scored a two, blocked a couple, but it was the fourth ball of the over that sent my off-stump spinning away down the field. I walked back to the marquee amidst a burst of desultory clapping, feeling rather relieved that I had done my turn for the rest of the day. It was now Reggie Tew's turn to go into bat. I could relax with the rest of the spectators. Raffles clapped me on the shoulder as I dropped into an empty canvas chair near him. 'Well done, Bunny,' he murmured. At least he knew my capabilities on the field.

Soon Reggie Tew and then Captain Walker were dismissed and Raffles went in as fifth man. He was soon totting up a respectable score. With the sexton's slow bowling he was able to strike out and place the ball wherever he wanted to send it, hitting fours and sixes all over the place. Off Larkin's bowling he was now and again able to achieve a four but more usually singles and byes. It was obvious at the rate he was scoring, Raffles was going to achieve his half-century before the vicar's wife and her ladies started to serve the strawberries and cream. Our victory seemed assured.

It was while he was facing Larkin's bowling that it happened. Larkin took his usual long run, came up to the stump like a snorting steam train, arm back. Raffles was presenting a straight bat. Larkin's arm started to describe an arc. Raffles moved forward slightly, bat raised. There was a crack. Raffles was standing like a statue but we could see his middle stump spinning. He turned slowly, looking round as if he could not believe it. The wicket-keeper had bent to pick it up – it was apparently in two pieces. The umpire, Tomkins, signalled for someone to bring out another stump.

I shuddered and thanked my lucky stars that I had survived those murderous balls from Larkin's hands. If they had the power to crack a stump in two then I daren't think what they would have done had I been struck on the person.

Raffles was striding back amid applause. I could see his lips were set in a thin line and there was a rather grim expression on his face. I have to confess that I was surprised. Even when bowled out Raffles had always maintained a sense of humour and never took such things seriously.

'Hard luck, old boy,' I began as he came striding up.

He frowned at me, suddenly seemed aware of his surroundings and forced a smile.

'Good show, old chap,' Lord Toby cried. 'Your innings has put them on the defensive. Look, can you keep an eye on things. I have to go up to the hall and get Fyson because he will have to go in soon. Dratted fellow said he'd forgotten some medicant for his asthma.'

Lord Toby turned and hurried away.

Raffles, as soon as he was out of earshot, hissed at me: 'Follow me, Bunny.'

I followed him around the side of the Marquee and stood watching as he took off his cricket pads.

'What's up, Raffles?'

'Where's Mackenzie?', he snapped.

'I think I saw him go into the White Bull for a drink. I say, I've never seen you in a tizzy about getting bowled out before.'

'Bowled out, my eye!' he snorted. 'Someone took a pot shot at me.'

'What?' I gasped.

Silently he held out his bat.

Towards its offside the wood seemed splintered and, just on the edge there was a small round hole, about the size of a sixpence, from which the splinters radiated.

'What's it mean?' I asked, perplexed.

'That's where the bullet struck. It passed through my bat and snapped my stump in two. The ball came past seconds later. I don't think Larkin nor his wicket-keeper saw it. They were too busy celebrating the fact that they thought I was bowled out.'

'Here, I say . . .' a fear suddenly seized me.

'Yes,' grunted Raffles. 'It means Fuchs is onto us.'

He peered round the marquee and glanced up towards a wooded hill a short way away. It was beyond this hill that the hall lay.

'Snap to it, Bunny,' cried Raffles. 'That's the direction from where the shot came and I mean to find out whose finger was on the trigger.'

'Hey!' I cried, as he began striding away. 'It's dangerous. Shouldn't I get Mackenzie?'

'Time is of the essence, Bunny,' cried Raffles. 'Quick's the word!'

Fearfully, I trailed behind him as he strode rapidly down the side of the cricket pitch towards the gently rising slopes of the hill. The hill was one of those typical South Downs foothills, a round, pudding shape on which was perched a cluster of trees. Raffles did not pause in his upward stride.

'Hey!' I gasped. 'Look there . . .'

A few hundred yards away, about a quarter of the way up the hill sat Reggie Tew, apparently availing himself of a grandstand seat to watch the cricket match. His gaze was on the match and he did not notice us.

'It must have been Reggie Tew. He's the only one up here,' I whispered.

Raffles shook his head.

'No. The trajectory is wrong, Bunny. The bullet must have been fired from those trees.'

'But it is rather coincidental that Reggie Tew is seated just there?' I said. 'No one else from the party is in a position to . . .'

'You forget our friend Fyson. Lord Toby said he had to go back to the hall to get some medicants for his asthma.'

I banged my fist into the palm of my other hand.

'Hush!' snapped Raffles. 'Let's go find out where the bullet was fired from.'

'What if the person who shot at you is still there?' I wheezed.

'I rather hope he is,' muttered Raffles grimly.

We reached the undergrowth surrounding the trees and, eyes searching warily, we followed the edge of the wood to a spot which looked down onto the field of play, exactly opposite the wicket where Raffles had been bowled out, or, rather, apparently bowled out. Cautiously, he pressed into the trees.

'The man is probably long gone,' he muttered.

Then he swooped down on the ground.

'By the Lord Harry, I was right.'

He stood up triumphantly holding a cartridge shell between thumb and forefinger.

'What do you make of that, Bunny?'

I bit my lip.

'It would seem as if Fuchs missed you.'

'That much is obvious,' returned Raffles sarcastically. 'What I meant was, what do you make of the cartridge?'

'It's not a sporting cartridge,' I ventured.

'Right! It's a precision bullet. I'd say it was used in a Lee-Enfield rifle.'

He pocketed the empty shell.

'We seem to have a professional rifleman with a good weapon at work here.'

He suddenly bent to the ground again.

'Our would-be assassin is a small man at that.'

I thought he was being dramatic.

'Oh come on, Raffles! How can you tell?'

'Elementary!' he said, pointing to the ground. I looked. It had been raining the previous night and, in spite of the scorching hot June day, the woods had shaded the ground and not allowed it to dry out properly. There were numerous footprints about, mainly of the same person it seemed. The imprints were of studded boots but of a small size.

'Not only is our man small, Bunny,' observed Raffles, 'but he has a distinct limp. See there, one imprint is heavier than the other.'

I started to congratulate him on his keen sight but he waved me to silence.

'I think we may be able to follow the bounder,' he said excitedly. 'There's a clear enough trail here.'

'Perhaps we ought to call Mackenzie?' I suggested.

'Let our man get away? No fear! Come on, Bunny, where's your spirit?'

He set off rapidly, following the footprints with me trailing reluctantly in the rear.

We had scarce pushed our way through the woods for a few minutes when we came to an abrupt halt on the edge of a small clearing. In the centre of the clearing was a small, rough wood shed, the sort that gamekeepers use for storing the bric-a-brac of their profession.

Raffles placed a finger over his lips.

The imprint of the boots led towards the door of the hut which was fastened. They did not lead away from it.

To my growing horror, Raffles crept stealthily towards the door and, with a cry, he afterwards told me was designed to paralyse his prey, he flung the door open and rushed in. I followed a split second later and bumped into Raffles. He was standing staring down at what, at first glance, seemed to be a heap of rags huddled almost in the doorway. On closer inspection I saw that it was the body of a man; a man of indeterminable age, dirty of face, with matted hair and beard and the clothes of a tramp. His

154

boots, though worn, were the only items of clothing not in an advanced state of decay.

He lay on his back, face upwards, eyes open and staring. Around his throat was a red, sticky substance.

It was only when I bent forward, puzzled, to see what it was that I realised that the man's throat had been cut.

CHAPTER TWENTY

I turned aside, trying hard to control my fluttering stomach. When I had recovered myself sufficiently I turned to find Raffles bending over the body and going through the pockets of the rags in which it was clad.

'I say, Bunny, look at this,' Raffles held up two golden guineas. 'That's an astonishing amount to find on a tramp and even more astonishing for any murderer to leave behind if robbery was the intention.'

Raffles was going through some papers creased in an old leather wallet.

'Our late lamented friend is one Jemmy Hardcastle,' he murmured. 'Apparently he was a corporal in the First East Kents, the Buffs, you know. Discharged unfit for duty having been wounded at Chitral. Poor fellow must have been hard up for work.'

I stared at Raffles in astonishment.

'Poor fellow? Isn't he the person who tried to kill you?'

'And answered the price of failure,' nodded Raffles. 'Two guineas, eh? It's rum to know what my life is worth.'

The realisation of what Raffles said sent a chill through me.

'You mean he was hired to kill you and when he failed, he was killed to stop him talking?'

'Something like that,' Raffles agreed blandly.

I looked around nervously.

'Then it could only have happened a few moments ago.'

'That's about right.'

'We'd better tell Mackenzie,' I ventured nervously.

'There's certainly nothing more that we can do here,' agreed Raffles.

He made to stand up and then, it seemed, his eye caught something. He bent over the body and then, taking a pocket handkerchief from his pocket, he pulled something out lying concealed under the man's jacket.

'It appears that the man who hired poor Corporal Hardcastle to eliminate me supplied him with the equipment which, as you have probably noticed, he has taken away with him. However, he has left this little item behind.'

I stared at the black gun metal object without comprehension. It reminded me of one piece of a pair of field glasses from which the lenses had been removed.

'What is it?' I asked.

'That, Bunny, is one of these new silencers. That explains why no one heard the report of the rifle.'

'You mean that thing deadens the sound of the report?'

'And, if I'm not much mistaken this is the handiwork of the firm of Mauser and Company.'

He pocketed the object, still keeping it wrapped in his handkerchief, along with Corporal Hardcastle's discharge papers and the two guineas.

'Let's get back to Mackenzie. He'll probably throw a fit at another murder.'

'If Mackenzie doesn't,' I said, 'I'm certainly about to.'

'Now then, Bunny,' cried Raffles, clapping me on the shoulder, 'hold fast! We are getting near our quarry. He's starting to make mistakes.'

I confessed that I could not see what mistakes the cold blooded Fuchs had committed so far.

Raffles smiled.

'He's getting into a tight corner, Bunny. We'll have him soon.'

Lord Toby was in batting when we returned and making a respectable showing. I noticed Reggie Tew was still sitting on the hillside apparently deeply interested in the game. And there was Fyson walking back from the direction of the hill. I scowled with my suspicions. Raffles walked along towards the marquee to where Mackenzie stood, puffing at an old briar pipe, and scowling at the match. Raffles stopped a few yards away from Mackenzie and made a surreptitious gesture with his eyes.

I take my hat off to Mackenzie. He caught the idea immediately and turned an expansive smile to Raffles.

'Excuse me, sir,' he said in his loudest Scots brogue, I'm a Scot, y'ken, and no verra knowledgable aboot yon game o' cricket. It's no a Scots game. Gie me a game the like o' shinty. Now there's a game for a man. But would ye be obligin' me to explain some points in yon game . . .?'

Even Raffles was hard pressed to suppress a smile at the man's acting.

In a low voice, as if explaining some points with constant gestures and nods towards the game in progress, Raffles told Mackenzie about the latest development. Mackenzie's face grew pale and worried.

'Then Fuchs is on to you?'

'So I think. As soon as the match is over Bunny and I will start for London. We may have a lead to follow but we will be in touch with you tomorrow.'

'Aye, and what'll I tell Sir Edward about developments?' growled Mackenzie. 'You been finding plenty o' bodies but no letters.'

'There will be some developments tomorrow, you can take my word for it,' Raffles assured him. Then he raised his voice: 'And you can see how a slow bowler can pitch to the best advantage.' He dropped his voice again. 'All I want you to do in the meantime, Mackenzie, is take this silencer and see if you can trace an owner or any fingerprints which might be on it.'

Mackenzie took the handkerchief wrapped object.

'I'll no promise about this new fangled fingerprinting. Ye canna beat old methods, old and tried and trusted, when it comes to detective work.'

He raised his hat and proclaimed loudly his thanks at Raffles information about cricket, observing that shinty was still a man's game and no Sassenach cricket would replace it.

Raffles and I passed into the White Bull and ordered two brandies.

There was a burst of clapping from the green. It seemed that Lord Toby had hit another six. If he could pull the trick twice more then we would be a run in advance and a wicket in hand. It was strange how this thought registered in my mind in spite of the recent events. We went and sat on a bench outside viewing the final moments of the game.

'This whole affair is becoming pretty nasty,' I said, breaking the silence.

'We knew it wasn't going to be easy, Bunny,' returned Raffles.

I swallowed my brandy nervously.

'If Fuchs is on to you, he'll be on to me as well,' I observed.

'Not necessarily. I believe that I was the one spotted returning from the summerhouse last night.'

'Spotted? By whom?'

'By Fuchs, of course. Fuchs knows or suspects that I am after him but he is not sure about you.'

'How do you make that out?'

'Because our late lamented friend from the Buffs would have been paid off to eliminate you too.'

I was not convinced.

'Anyway, Bunny,' went on Raffles, 'I'm a marked man. It's no use me going to Hyde Park tomorrow because if I am seen strolling near Rotten Row, Fuchs will immediately go to ground.'

'Don't you think he will anyway after all this excitement?'

'He might chance it so, I'm afraid, you are going to station yourself at the appointed place and see what happens. Then you hoof it back to Albany for all you're worth.'

'But if Fuchs suspects me he won't show anyway,' I protested.

'That's something that we will have to chance.'

'It seems to me that I'll be doing all the chancing,' I protested.

'Oh, buck up Bunny . . .'

'Harry!'

Clarissa Walker came over with a scolding look on her pretty features.

'You've been neglecting me most shamefully this afternoon, Harry,' she pouted.

I reddened and mumbled something.

With a cynical smile Raffles rose to his feet and excused himself. Clarissa sat down next to me. I looked round nervously.

'Don't worry about Harold,' she said coldly. 'He's taken a bottle of whisky and gone back to the hall.'

'Oh I say . . .' I said sympathetically.

She pouted.

'And when I looked around for you, you were nowhere to be seen. I really didn't think you were the sort of man, Harry Manders, who took advantage of a lady and then just cast her aside like a used napkin.'

A small voice urged me to say that if anyone had been taken advantage of it was me. But I silenced it and took her hand.

'I say, Clarissa, I'm most frightfully sorry.'

She appeared a little mollified.

'Where have you been?'

'Er, why, er, the call of nature,' I ended lamely.

'You seem frightfully friendly with that Mister Roberts.'

'Roberts?' I was nearly caught off guard. 'Oh yes,' I said hurriedly. 'I knew him at school and we served in the Boer War together.'

'Oh? You're a close friend then?'

I shrugged.

'Well,' I said being truthful, 'I haven't seen the fellow for nearly four years. Not since the Boer War, actually. Last saw him at Kimberly in 1900. Then, a few days ago, I bumped into him again in London.'

Clarissa smiled at me.

'You must have been awfully brave to serve in the war.'

I smiled modestly.

'Not really. A chap had to do what was expected of him.

Raf . . . er, my friend, won the Distinguished Service Cross.'

'Is he still in the army?'

'Good Lor' no!' I smiled. 'Gentleman of leisure.' I tried hard to think of a suitable profession for Raffles. 'He's interested in collecting antique gold and silver,' I said truthfully.

'So you haven't seen him for years?' pressed Clarissa. 'Is that why you're spending so much time in his company and neglecting me?'

'I really didn't mean to neglect you, Clarissa,' I mumbled.

She smiled.

'Silly boy! Go and buy me a sherry and let's plan what we are going to do next weekend after my beastly husband has departed on his rotten safari into the Kalahari or wherever the rotten place is.'

Clarissa Walker had some definite views on what she wanted to do that following weekend and most of her ideas did not involve moving out of her house.

These plans were interrupted by a sudden burst of applause. Lord Toby, it seemed, was in fine form and every ball that Larkin or his colleague, the sexton, sent down, was returned for a four or six. The game was over. We had won by five runs with a wicket still in hand. It was about five o'clock when we all trooped into the marquee for a splendid tea which I never felt less like eating. We all returned to the hall by seven o'clock that evening.

It seemed that all the guests were departing for London in various forms of transport. The German party left almost immediately in their touring car. I smiled cynically, for it was the car that von Heumann was supposed to have used to get back to London and here it was mysteriously ready to take the ambassador and his guests back. In retrospect, this was rather an oversight in Fuchs' meticulous planning. But nobody sought to question the fact perhaps due to the hustle and bustle of the departure. I noticed that Raffles bade Baroness von Stalhein a rather fond farewell before their departure.

Reggie Tew had a car and gave the Walkers a lift with

Doctor Fyson. Captain Walker had to be helped into the car in a deplorable state, still clutching a three-quarters empty bottle of whisky. Clarissa shot me a smile and mouthed 'Next weekend' when no one was looking. Every one else departed by the various means in which they had arrived. Even Lord Toby said he was travelling back to London that evening because he had important business to transact first thing in the morning.

Lord Toby's groom, Charles, drove us back to Horsham station in time for us to catch the nine o'clock fast train into Victoria. Raffles offered to put me up for the night but I decided to get a room at the Reform Club and so he dropped me there with some final instructions about my morning's adventure before instructing the Hansom to proceed to Albany.

I gave orders that I was to be roused at five o'clock to give me time to get across to Hyde Park by six o'clock. I was not looking forward to the adventure. Spying had turned into an absolutely beastly game. Everywhere one turned there were dead bodies lying about. I could not believe Raffles' assurances that Fuchs might think that I had no professional connection with Raffles. It seemed a slender chance. Personally, I was sure that Fuchs, and in my estimation Fuchs and Fyson were one and the same, would not turn up in Rotten Row in the morning.

Doctor Seward Fyson was Fuchs.

The more I thought about it, the more I became sure of it.

CHAPTER TWENTY-ONE

I had been waiting in Rotten Row since six o'clock and it was now approaching nine o'clock. I was stiff, bored and rather annoyed with the whole business. I had been walking up and down, impatient and anxious and there was still no sign of the mysterious Fuchs. I had not observed anything remotely suspicious. Fed up, I took up a new stand near the Albert Gate end of the Row. There were quite a number of people in the park now, and a dozen or so ladies and gentlemen on horseback galloping up and down.

'Harry, old fellow! What the devil are you doing here?'

I turned and bit my lip in annoyance. It was my brother-in-law, Lord Toby, dressed in a garish tweed suit and walking stick, advancing towards me.

'Good Lor', Harry, I didn't realise that you went in for morning constitutionals.'

I greeted him, perhaps a little surlily, and asked him what he was doing in Hyde Park at that hour.

'Arranged to meet Doctor Fyson here,' he returned easily. 'Business appointment. Fellow said he had to pass by this way and I felt I could do with a bit of a constitutional . . . weekends in the country make me feel quite vigorous.'

I felt a growing satisfaction.

Fyson, my prime suspect, was running true to form.

Lord Toby was looking at his watch.

'Fellow should be here soon,' he muttered.

I started to look round. I didn't want to miss the moment when Fyson made contact with his courier. Immediately I noticed a tall man in uniform enter the Albert Gate and stand peering round. He looked nervous and ill at ease. It was his uniform that made me gape at the man. It was rather a resplendent one. Now I'm usually a bit of a duffer at deciphering one uniform from another but there was no mistaking the national origin of this one. The black polished riding boots, the immaculately cut short jacket, a black cross medal at the throat and a pickelhaube helmet to crown it. It was the uniform of an officer in the Imperial German Army. Was this the courier? It had to be.

Lord Toby was rambling on about the weekend and how pleasant the thing had been while I stood watching the German officer trying to suppress my excitement.

'Ah,' exclaimed Lord Toby, 'here comes Fyson now.'

My heart lurched as the tall, bearded figure of Doctor Seward Fyson swung through the gate. He walked with a purposeful stride. I found myself holding my breath. Sure enough, the German officer turned at his approach. He stepped forward and Fyson halted. Fyson's hand went to his pocket and drew something out. I could not see what passed between them. Then the German officer turned and was walking rapidly away while Fyson came on into the park.

What would Raffles do? My mind was in a panic.

It was now clear to me beyond all doubt that Fyson was 'The Fox', the mysterious Fuchs. He had kept his appointment with the courier. Should I now accuse Fyson in front of Lord Toby? No; that would not get the letters back. It was our task to retrieve those letters at all costs before they were spirited away to Germany. That had to be my first consideration. I turned abruptly to my brother-in-law:

'Excuse me, old chap. I've just realised that I'm frightfully late for an appointment.'

Courtesy demanded that I raise my hat as I strode past Fyson, if only to allay any suspicions. He gave me a curious glance, nodded, but Lord Toby's effusive greeting prevented him paying further attention to me. I set off in hot pursuit of the disappearing German officer.

'Manders!'

A figure appeared directly in my path. It was the abominable Reggie Tew looking as spruce as ever and sporting a pince-nez.

'Absolutely topping to see you, old fellow. Didn't know you frequented these parts. Always stroll here myself. I say . . .'

I moved agitatedly out of his way.

'Haven't a moment to spare, Reggie,' I snapped. 'Must dash, urgent appointment. See you soon.'

I pushed by him and hurried after the distant figure of the German officer.

I congratulated myself on my ability to sleuth for I was able to keep up with the man as he made his way out of the park by Apsley House and hail a Hansom at the bottom of Park Lane. I looked round desperately. As luck would have it a cab was trotting by and I leapt aboard. Judging by the way the driver did not even bat an eyelid, I assumed that it was a natural occurrence for breathless men to fling themselves in cabs and demand drivers to chase other cabs. The German's Hansom turned along Piccadilly and then up Shaftesbury Avenue. At Cambridge Circus it turned down Earlham Street to the Seven Dials and then into Shelton Street where it halted before a block of seedy looking tenements. The block was one of those strange constructions which gave ingress to the various apartments from the outside of the building by means of iron stairways and iron-railed balconies which ran entirely round the building on each floor.

I was surprised by the immaculately clad German officer's destination. It did not look the sort of place that any self-respecting foreigner, let alone a member of the Imperial German Army Officer Corps, would choose to stay. I paid off my cabby and followed the man as he climbed the stairs to a first floor balcony, walked along it and halted outside a door, fumbling for keys. He obviously had no idea that he had been followed for he never once glanced in my direction as I walked up behind him.

'Got you!' I shouted in triumph, grabbing him by the shoulder.

Instead of turning on me, the burly German seemed to collapse and make a half hearted attempt to wriggle from my grasp.

' 'Swelp me, guv'nor, I *h*aint done nuffin' wrong!'

The whining Cockney voice disconcerted me for a moment, so much that I nearly let go of the man. I stared at the German officer in amazement. He was certainly not my idea of a *korrekt* Prussian officer. Good sense made me hang onto the fellow otherwise I dare say he would have scuttled away down the nearest alley.

'Who the devil are you?' I demanded.

'Bert Small, guv'nor.'

'And what do you mean, dressing up in that uniform?'

'I'm *h*an *h*actor.'

'An actor?' I smiled grimly. 'And what part are you playing now? What were you doing in Rotten Row dressed as a German officer?'

'Swelp me, *h*aint done nuffin' wrong,' he whined again. 'You the rozzers?'

'No, I'm not the police but let us say that I am not unknown at New Scotland Yard,' I replied truthfully.

'Gawd!' breathed Bert Small. 'The gennelman said it were all legal like. I *h*aint done nuffin' wrong.'

I was growing weary of his repetition.

'Let's go inside then you'd better tell me about it.'

Reluctantly, the man produced his latch key, opened his door and we entered. He took off his pickelhaube helmet and set it down, loosening his jacket. I stood near the door and watched while the man nervously poured himself a beer but declined when he proffered the bottle to me.

'Well?'

'*H*its like this 'ere, guv'nor. I does mainly music 'all turns, you knows the type o' thing? But *h*i've *h*also done bit parts 'ere and there. Naw lawst *h*evening this gennelman knocks me door and arsks as 'ow *h*i'd likes ter *h*earn a fiver. Naw I bin awt o' work fer a couple o' months, guv', but strŏight *h*up I arsks whevver it were legal an' *h*all. The gennelman sez as 'ow it were. *H*all I 'ad ter do was 'ire this 'ere suit from Crawford's the Costumier in Drury Lane and be *h*at *h*Albert Gate in Rotten Row at nine this morning.'

He paused to take a swallow of his beer.

'What then?' I prompted.

'The gennelman described another gennelman to me who, 'e sez, would come along abawt that time. When 'e did, I was to approach 'im, salute and say: *Entschuldigen Sie bitte, Wie spät ist es?*'

I started in surprise.

'You speak German?'

'Bless yer, naw!' he grinned. 'I'm *h*an *h*actor, *h*aint I? The gennelman tells me the dialogue and I remembers *h*it parrot fashion.'

'Very well, go on.'

'Whatever the man says to me, I am to reply: *Danke, Auf Wiedersehen.*'

'What if the man tries to talk further with you?'

'Then I was to say: *Ich habe es eilig* and hurry away. But that didn't 'appen, guv'nor. It *h*all went like clockwork . . . till you showed up.'

I was halfway between rage and admiring the cool, deadly proficiency of Fuchs. Having realised that his contact might be observed, he had laid on such a clever diversion. He had hired an actor to impersonate a rather obvious German officer, given him some lines to learn in order to accost Doctor Fyson and ask him for the time. When given, the man would make the correct response. If Fyson pressed the matter further, the pseudo German would merely excuse himself and hurry off. From a distance, the drama would appear as though Fyson had made contact with his courier and handed over the letters. I cursed myself for being such a fool. Surely this meant that Fyson was innocent? Unless . . . unless Fuchs was so deuced clever that he *was* Fyson and making an effort to put suspicion elsewhere.

'What a bloody fool!' I echoed my thoughts aloud.

'Wot's *h*up, guv'nor?' demanded the actor anxiously. 'I *h*aint done nuffin' wrong, 'as I?'

I picked up the pickelhaube helmet. Inside was the label: Crawford's Theatrical Costumes, Drury Lane.

'No,' I sighed. 'Did you get your fiver?'

'*H*in *h*advance,' grinned Bert Small smugly. 'And the money for the 'ire of the costume.'

It was then I suddenly remembered something. If Fyson *was* in the clear who else was a likely suspect? Reggie Tew! By God, Raffles had been suspicious of him from the very start. He had been at Rotten Row that morning. I turned to Bert Small eagerly.

'This chap who hired you, was he German or English?'

'Couldn't rightly say. Seemed English, guv'nor. Bit of a toff like yourself.'

'Can you describe him?'

'Not *h*exactly,' Bert Small pondered. ''e was a little above your 'eight dressed in *h*an *h*ulster and 'at the 'ole time. Reckons I know 'im agin though.'

I nearly hugged the man. At least my chase had not been in vain. We now had someone who had met Fuchs face to face and was able to recognise him.

'You are coming with me, Bert Small,' I told him, trying to keep the excitement out of my voice.

'I *h*aint done nuffin' wrong, guv'nor!'

'Say that again and I'll strangle you,' I returned. 'You have just volunteered to help your country in time of crisis, and I don't doubt that you will double or treble your fiver to boot.'

Bert Small grinned.

'Naw yer talkin' guv'nor. Give me 'alf a mo' ter change awt of these rags into some'in' respectable.'

I nodded and spent the next couple of minutes examining the posters, pinned round the walls of the room, which announced Bert Small's music hall credits.

'Ready, guv'nor.'

Bert Small, clad in a rather worn but passable suit, stood ready.

'Let's go,' I said, letting him precede me out of the door onto the balcony.

He was standing aside to let me through so that he could relock the door when there was a soft 'phutt!' and he started, turned towards me with an open mouth, and slowly collapsed to the doorstep. Not understanding for a moment, I bent to catch him. It was then I saw the tiny red mark near his right temple. It was the act of bending down that saved my life. There was another soft 'phutt' from nearby and something splintered the wood of the door above my head.

I went cold with fear.

Someone had shot Bert Small. Someone was now trying to kill me! I dragged the body of the tall Cockney inside the room and slammed the door shut. Still hopeful, I bent over the actor and felt for his heart. I knew really before I touched him that it was no use. He was dead. Shot through the brain.

Damn, but Fuchs was a clever devil. He had not only drawn me away from the rendezvous by his ruse but had followed us up to make sure that Bert Small could not identify him. Now the cold blooded devil was trying to kill me. Well, Harry Manders was not going to hang

167

around with a corpse waiting for Fuchs to knock on the door. I glanced around Bert Small's room. At the back there was a window. I made my way over to it and peered out. My luck was in and I thanked the person who had designed this tenement block. A balcony and fire-escape system ran down the back of the building. Praying that Fuchs had some flaws in his knowledge, I hauled up the window and made my way down to the back yard. From here it was an easy matter to negotiate my way into a back street and walk rapidly towards a main road, leaping aboard the first tram-car to trundle down it.

My first call in central London was at New Scotland Yard where Mackenzie listened gravely to my story.

'I knew it wouldna be easy wi' you and Raffles turned polismen,' muttered the Scot with a shake of his head. 'Bodies, bodies, bodies all over the place and what's to show for it?'

'That's unfair,' I retorted, annoyed. 'Raffles and I are risking our lives to track down this cold blooded fellow.'

'Aye, and that's no great loss I'm thinking.'

He leant back with a nasty smile.

'I make six bodies to date and no solution to the problem. I ask you Mister Manders, how many more bodies do you intend to deposit with us before you have finished?'

I snorted indignantly and stood up.

'I suggest you send your men to Bert Small's room before the local police make the affair public,' I said as I left the ungracious Detective Chief Superintendent.

Thoroughly exhausted with my morning's adventures I reached Albany about lunchtime and immediately went up to Raffles' rooms. I knocked on the door and tried it, but it was locked. Usually, when Raffles is in it is a little habit of his to leave the door unlocked so that he can just sing out to whoever comes by to enter. I was about to turn away, believing him to be out, when my ears caught a scuffling sound behind the door and whispered voices. I stood hesitantly. Then came the sound of the catch being lifted and the door opened a few inches. There was Raffles peering out at me, rather red in the face, so I thought.

'Raffles, old man . . .' I began.

'Hush,' he returned, looking curiously embarrassed.

'What's up?' I asked, lowering my tone to match his.

'Can you come back in twenty minutes, old chap?'

Puzzled, I nodded.

There was a pleading look in Raffles' eye.

Nearly opposite Albany stands Bewley's Tea Shop and so, wondering what was up, I crossed Piccadilly and took a seat by the window of that establishment. I ordered some toasted muffins and tea and sat down to wait. Fifteen minutes later the mystery was cleared up when out of the Albany doors came the elegant figure of a woman. It was the Baroness von Stalhein. I did not even speculate where, among the inhabitants of Albany, she was paying a call. I swallowed my tea, paid my bill, and returned to Raffles' rooms.

'Sorry about that, Bunny,' he greeted me rather bashfully. 'I had a visitor.'

'So I saw,' I returned.

'I've been pursuing my own line of enquiry.'

'I've no doubt,' I said dryly, flinging myself on his Chesterfield. 'In the meantime, I've nearly been killed. I was shot at.'

Raffles' eyes widened.

'Tell me what happened.'

I spared no detail.

He leant back and lit a Sullivan.

'So, we are no closer to discovering the identity of Fuchs,' he said, after a while.

'We could eliminate Fyson, I suppose,' I suggested. 'On the other hand Fuchs has shown himself to be so clever that the whole charade with Bert Small could have been planned by Fyson to throw suspicion on to someone else. No, I don't think we are any further forward. And the letters might be on their way out of the country already.'

'No.' Raffles said it so emphatically that I gave him a curious look. He smiled. 'The Baroness has been rather co-operative, old chap. Fuchs has to work to a timetable.'

He suddenly drew out a piece of paper, flourishing it

with the air of a conjurer producing a rabbit.

'Read that, Bunny.'

It was a telegraph addressed to the Baroness. It was laconic to say the least. '*Seig Boot. Mitternach. Mittwoch. F.*' 'Victory Boat. Midnight. Wednesday. F.' I translated aloud.

I turned to Raffles.

'What does it mean?'

'It is from Fuchs. A final communication to the Baroness letting her know where and when the letters will be taken out of the country.'

I was astonished.

'The Baroness gave it to you?'

'Let us say I borrowed it,' smiled Raffles.

I had to admire the man.

'What does it mean, though?' I repeated.

'We know the letters were to be taken out of the country by a courier and Fuchs has to hand the letters to that courier. The letters are obviously leaving the country at midnight on Wednesday.'

'By a "Victory Boat"? What's that.'

'It's a form of shorthand, Bunny. Where do most continental boat trains leave from?'

I frowned.

'Why, Victoria Station . . . Victoria, *Victory*! Good Lord!'

'Thanks to the Baroness, we have the information of exactly where and when the letters will leave for Germany. We must be on that boat train at midnight, Wednesday. It will be our last chance to stop Fuchs and his henchmen.'

CHAPTER TWENTY-TWO

Raffles and I arrived at Victoria Railway Station at half-past-eleven. Although the main concourse of the station was fairly deserted there was a lot of activity on and around the platform from which the midnight boat train was due to leave. Of course, it was summer and a number of families were going to the seaside. Porters wheeled baggage to and fro, and attendants glanced at tickets and escorted passengers to their compartments in the impatiently puffing train on which a large sign proclaimed its destination:

London–Dover–Calais–Paris.

Raffles shoved our tickets towards a blue uniformed attendant.

'Good evening, gentlemen,' the man said, glancing at the tickets. 'You will find plenty of room towards the centre of the train.'

Raffles smiled acknowledgement and we pushed our way through the throng, laying claim to a small first class compartment which was empty.

Raffles collapsed in a corner, took out his silver cigarette case, extracted a Sullivan and sent the smoke in expanding circles to the ceiling.

'Ah,' he sighed, 'that's better.'

To my astonishment he suddenly stood up and commenced to pull down all the blinds thus secluding the compartment from outside inspection but also preventing us from observing the crowds.

'We don't want our German friends to spot us before the train moves off, do we?' he said, seeing my astonishment.

'What's your plan, Raffles?'

'As soon as the train pulls out, we shall make a thorough search of it. If my suspicions are correct, we will find not merely the courier but Fuchs himself. It's my guess that Fuchs realises that the net is closing in on him in England and that he is personally taking these letters to Berlin.'

I gasped.

'Then you know who it is?' I said accusingly.

Raffles smiled.

'I suspect, Bunny, which is less than knowing.'

Certainly Raffles had been behaving oddly during the last twenty-four hours and had spent some considerable time in the company of Mackenzie.

'Was it anything to do with those telegrams Mackenzie brought round to the Albany this evening?' I prompted.

'All will be revealed in good time, Bunny,' said Raffles smoothly.

Just then the carriage door sprang back and a fat little man with a great walrus moustache wedged himself in the doorway.

Raffles peered up with a haughty expression.

'This compartment is reserved,' he said coldly.

The little man looked round apologetically.

'Sorry, mister,' his voice betrayed his north country origin.

'Aint there room in there, father?' came a shrill woman's voice across his shoulder.

The little man tried to back out.

'It's reserved, mother,' he said in a rather ingratiating voice.

'Garn!' came the shrill tone. 'You can't reserve third class.'

'This happens to be first class,' I snorted. 'You are obviously in the wrong part of the train.'

The little man gave a hopeless shrug and pushed himself backwards. I pushed the door shut but we could still hear the woman's shrill and aggrieved tones echoing along the corridor.

A whistle blew and there came a long, melancholy answer from the engine.

Raffles drew back a corner of the blind and peered out.

'We're off,' he said.

I peered over his shoulder through the chink onto the platform. We were not quite off.

A whistle sounded again.

There was a sudden jerk and the long lighted platform began to slide slowly past the window.

The train was moving forward.

In a moment Raffles stood up.

'Right, Bunny,' he said briskly. 'Keep your wits about you. The game we are after is an armed and dangerous one.'

My mouth went dry.

'I think our best bet is to go forward and work our way back.'

'Do you really know who we are looking for?' I pressed him as we stepped into the corridor.

'Fairly certain of it, old chap.'

'Dash it, Raffles, can't you give a fellow some idea?'

He shook his head.

'If I'm wrong, I'd prefer to keep my mistakes to myself.'

We began to inch along the swaying corridor, now and then peering into compartments but no faces were familiar to me. As we moved through a third class compartment I caught sight of the little man with the walrus moustache, still trying to settle his shrill voiced wife. He grinned apologetically as we passed by.

We moved into a first class carriage. I was leading the way at the time when, as I chanced to glance down into a compartment, I came face to face with my brother-in-law, Lord Toby Devenish. I made to draw back, realising that he was the last person we wanted to get involved with while engaged in the search for Fuchs. It was too late. He saw me and sprang up with a smile of greeting to open the compartment door.

'By the Lord Harry! What are you doing on the train, old chap? You do crop up in the most amazing places, these days.'

I hesitated.

'I, er, that is, I'm going to visit Alice in Paris,' I blurted in a flash of inspiration.

Lord Toby peered over my shoulder.

'Why, if it isn't your friend, Mister Raffles.'

'Hello, Devenish,' Raffles greeted him in a quiet voice.

'So you are off to Paris, eh? That's exactly where I am heading. Jove, what a coincidence. Come on in,' he motioned us into his compartment. 'I've a flask of brandy here, never travel without it.'

I started to make an excuse but, to my surprise, Raffles pushed me forward.

'That's kind of you, Devenish.'

I frowned: what the devil was Raffles playing at? We had to search the train for Fuchs and not waste the time of day, or rather night, with my brother-in-law.

Raffles voice suddenly came harshly in my ears.

'I wouldn't do that if I were you, Herr Fuchs!'

Lord Toby was standing in a frozen position, his hand towards his coat pocket. He turned and forced a smile, shrugged and sat down, staring up at Raffles.

'Harry, old chap, perhaps you can explain what your friend means?' he asked quietly.

I had begun to splutter.

'Look here . . .' I started but Raffles waved me to silence.

'Bunny, I think it is high time you met Herr Fuchs, the code name for the head of German intelligence in England. Lord Toby Devenish.'

I let my mouth hang open.

'You . . . you can't mean that, Raffles?' I gasped, trying to recover my wits. 'Hang it, the fellow is Alice's brother.'

I had never seen Raffles so deadly serious before.

'Oh, but I do mean it, Bunny.'

Lord Toby had a curious expression on his face. He attempted to chuckle.

'Your friend is a little mad, Harry.'

Raffles smiled grimly.

'As I said before, Devenish, the game is up. Do you want an explanation, Bunny?'

I felt weak and collapsed in a corner seat.

Raffles sat down in the opposite corner, his black eyes fixed firmly on Lord Toby.

'Yesterday, as you know, I spent some time with our good friend Mackenzie. We were doing some research. I became suspicious of Lord Toby during the weekend. Let's start from the beginning. He was once in the Foreign Office, spoke fluent German and was an attaché in Berlin for some years. When he inherited the title, he resigned from the Foreign Office and returned to England. But the Devenish estates were mortgaged up to the hilt. The Devenish family were actually paupers. Yet, within a few months, Lord Toby was able to buy off all the mortgages on Hurstdevenish as well as the Devenish town house, able to buy a shooting lodge in Scotland and a villa outside of Monte Carlo, and provide a very comfortable income for his sister and himself. On returning from Berlin he ceased to be a pauper and became a comfortable man about town. How was it done?'

There was a silence.

For the first time I realised that my brother-in-law's face was deathly white. The skin was drawn tight around his mouth.

'How?' I urged slowly.

'Mackenzie had to throw his weight around with Devenish's bank manager and lawyer. They told us that Lord Toby had spoken of several large wins at the casinos in Baden-Baden and Monte Carlo. That did not seem likely. Telegrams were sent off to the casinos and the answers arrived this evening.'

I nodded, remembering Mackenzie arriving at the Albany with a sheaf of cables whose contents seemed a source of satisfaction.

Raffles leant forward.

'No such wins were ever made at the casinos by Lord Toby. Where had this money come from?'

'It doesn't mean Lord Toby was paid by German Intelligence,' I pointed out. 'In fact, Raffles, nothing you've said is conclusive proof that Toby is Fuchs.'

'No,' admitted Raffles, 'but accepting, however, things in logical sequence there is a case to be answered. Fuchs was at Lord Toby's weekend party. Let us suppose Lord Toby is Fuchs.

'Poor Cartwright overhears Toby and von Heumann discussing plans to hand over the letters in Rotten Row. Toby leaves and von Heumann discovers Cartwright. They fight and somehow manage to kill each other, except that Cartwright lives long enough to pass some information on to you, Bunny. The only thing he isn't able to pass on is the identity of Fuchs.'

Raffles paused, pulled out his silver cigarette case, extracted a Sullivan and lit it.

There was no sound in the compartment save the jogging and rattling of the train.

He exhaled and smiled thinly at Lord Toby.

'You, Bunny, call me from the ballroom and we return to the summer house where this has taken place. But the bodies have gone. Fuchs has removed them. When I return from the summer house, I am seen by Fuchs. Now who did I meet on my way back?'

I frowned.

'Reggie Tew, Doctor Fyson and . . .'

'And Lord Toby,' ended Raffles. 'Fuchs or Lord Toby knows that I am on to him. He tries to eliminate me. At the cricket match he hires a down at heel ex-serviceman to kill me. The man misses. Lord Toby or Fuchs has to eliminate the man. He leaves the field, ostensibly to go after Fyson who, he says, has returned to the house to get his asthma medicants. By the time we reach the would-be assassin, Lord Toby has done the job.'

My mouth sagged wider.

'You don't mean, Toby . . .?'

'By a fluke,' went on Raffles, ignoring my unasked question, 'Fyson and Reggie Tew provided some red herrings for us. Even on Monday morning in Rotten Row, Fyson and Reggie Tew were there. More importantly, so was Lord Toby already having arranged a distraction. He arranged that little pantomime simply to draw us out in the open. He knew I was after him and he wanted to make sure of you.'

Raffles laughed.

'Suffering Icarus, Bunny. You really fell for it. What would a German, complete in riding boots and pickelhaube helmet, be doing strolling around London? Your rapid departure after the Judas-goat confirmed that you were working with me. Lord Toby realised that the net was closing in. He decided to take the letters in person to his masters in the Wilhelmstrasse so that he could demand that they set him up in a nice apartment in Berlin. But he had to let the surviving member of his group know and so he sent a laconic note to the Baroness informing her that he was leaving the country and from where and when.'

Raffles grinned.

'Don't you find it odd, Lord Toby, that Baroness von Stalhein has not joined you?'

Lord Toby grimaced but said nothing.

'The game's up, Fuchs,' there was a harsh note in Raffles' voice.

'I don't think so,' returned Lord Toby evenly. 'You've told a very interesting tale but it's a story that won't stand up without some hard proof.'

Raffles grinned.

'Such as the letters you have secreted on your person? There will be a little reception committee waiting for us when we get to Dover. I think the letters which you carry will be more than enough proof.'

'And another thing,' I said as the thought occurred to me. 'How did you know he was Raffles? As you greeted us just now you called him "Mister Raffles" when all the time he has been known to you as Roberts.'

Lord Toby gave me a pitying look and laughed. It was a chilling sound.

'Very well, gentlemen. But there is one thing that you have entirely wrong. I was just a minor cog in the network. Why, Fuchs is not even a man.'

We stared at him in astonishment.

'Come in, darling, and cover them.'

The compartment door slid open and a tiny derringer pistol pointed unwaveringly towards Raffles and me. It was held in the tiny begloved hand of an attractive woman.

I gaped.

177

It was Clarissa Walker.

'Sit absolutely still, Mister Raffles,' she snapped in a hard voice as she entered the compartment and slid the door shut behind her. 'And for God's sake, Harry, stop catching flies in your mouth.'

I tried to draw my teeth together.

'Gentlemen, allow me to introduce Frau Fuchs,' chuckled Lord Toby.

'Clarissa . . . I don't understand?' I stammered.

'You boob!' she said scornfully. 'You don't really understand much, do you?'

I turned crimson.

'You two are not all-knowing, after all,' Lord Toby was grinning. 'You've only stumbled on half the story. True, you've discovered enough to embarrass us but you might as well hear it all since you'll never be in a position to repeat it. I was merely co-ordinator of our network while Frau Klara Fuchs was the chief. We began to suspect you two when we realised that Harry, here, was making rather a lot of trips down to the White Bull to see Mister Cleophane of Dundee, who turned out to be none other than a senior Scotland Yard man. Frau Fuchs, or Clarissa if you prefer, decided to take Harry in hand, to try and find out what game he was about. I must say she did it rather well.'

I stared at Clarissa's cold face. Her mouth drooped.

'I didn't even have the satisfaction of finding you good in bed,' she said nastily.

I could have killed her in that instant.

Lord Toby laughed uproarously.

'What of Captain Walker?' asked Raffles curiously.

'That dolt!' sneered Clarissa. 'When I came to England three years ago to take up my role, I needed a cover so I married him. He knows nothing. All he is interested in is his ridiculous safaris.'

'Two years ago Clarissa became my chief,' said Lord Toby, 'not to mention my mistress. We had an excellent network going until you blundered along.'

Raffles was nodding as if understanding was dawning.

'Of course! Cartwright!' He looked at Clarissa. 'You

killed Cartwright, didn't you? I knew sticking a meat cleaver in him was not the sort of trick von Heumann would play. He was too much of an officer. It had to be a woman.'

'Cartwright was a fool,' sneered Clarissa. 'He betrayed himself in several ways. We would have dealt with him before had it not been for the fact that Harry was suspicious about him and started to ask questions. We wondered whether Cartwright was working for someone else. Then we discovered that the Secret Service, not trusting you two to deliver the goods, placed another man, Cartwright, in the house without telling you.'

'But Cartwright was killed just after you left me,' I protested.

'Von Heumann had met Toby in the library and Toby had told him that he would have to hand the documents to a courier in Rotten Row for despatch to Berlin. As I returned from you to the ballroom I saw Cartwright hovering by the door. He saw me and sped upstairs. The fool must have gone to warn you or Raffles. I told Toby and von Heumann. Toby had to get back to the guests but von Heumann and I went round the back of the house, meaning to sneak up on Cartwright. While von Heumann went to deal with him I went into the summer house to arrange some sacking in which to hide the body.'

I stared at her cold blooded recitation.

'The next thing I saw was Cartwright stumbling into the summer house as if being pursued. He was, von Heumann was chasing him. Cartwright turned and fired at von Heumann and killed him. I seized an old meat cleaver which was lying on a bench in the summer house and stabbed him. Then I ran out to tell Toby.'

Lord Toby nodded.

'I took care of the rest. We also had to eliminate you. But too many bodies about the house was not a good thing. The next day we arranged Mister Raffles' assassination. The idea was to be a revenge killing by an old soldier with a grudge for a former officer. The assassin was going to take his own life. It didn't work out. The pantomime at Rotten Row was not meant to act as camouflage for the act of handing over the documents. We had already decided to take the letters to Germany ourselves. It was merely to eliminate one or both of you in surroundings of our own choice. Again, it didn't work.'

Clarissa nodded.

'And now we are on our way to the Fatherland. You shall not stop us.'

'They have arrested the Baroness,' Lord Toby pointed out.

'Then she must fend for herself,' replied Clarissa.

'Very well. I'm sorry, gentlemen,' Lord Toby smiled evenly. 'The time has come when you must get off the train.'

'You utter beasts!' I cried, staring from his amused face to the cold sneering expression of Clarissa Walker.

I don't know. Something seemed to snap inside of me. Perhaps it was the shame and outrage which Clarissa Walker had made me feel. I suddenly sprang towards her and seized the wrist which held the derringer, with both hands. The struggle lasted only a matter of seconds. She clung determinedly to the small pistol, struggling to point it towards my heart and fire. Gradually I sought to turn her aim away from me. She must have been clenching hard on the trigger for there came a muffled explosion and a dark red stain began to spread over the breast of her costume. She gave a groan and fell limply in my arms.

I was still numb with shock when Lord Toby sprang for the door of the compartment, opened it and jumped onto the running board, hands grasping the door handles as he started to edge his way along the outside of the carriage.

Raffles moved with equal alacrity and was after his man in a trice.

For some moments I stood there, gaping first at the dead body of Clarissa Walker and then at the open, swinging door as air and engine smoke swirled passed me at a furious rate. I could see the dark banks and trees of the night countryside, with the occasional light flashing by. Trying to recover myself, I laid Clarissa's body on the seats and edged over to the door.

My heart was in my mouth as I peered out. I could see the dark figure of Lord Toby crawling his way upwards to the roof of the carriage. There was Raffles in hot pursuit.

I stood helpless, not knowing what to do.

My circling eyes caught sight of the communication cord with its red lettered warning about unauthorised use. I reached forward and yanked with all my might.

For some seconds nothing happened. I could hear the noises on the roof of the compartment, scuffling sounds as Lord Toby and Raffles struggled for supremacy. Then I thought I heard a cry. As I stood staring out of the door, wondering what else I could do, I saw two dark shapes, clasped together, hurl by into the night.

I nearly fainted with shock.

Raffles and Lord Toby had fallen from the train in their struggle.

CHAPTER TWENTY-THREE

The brakes of the train were now squealing in protest, the engine slowing down with a series of jerks. Then came a silence only broken by the hissing of the engine.

The door of the compartment crashed open.

I stared uncomprehendingly as the little man with the walrus moustache pushed in, a revolver clasped in one hand. His eyes grimly took in the body of Clarissa Walker, the open compartment door, swinging idly in the dark night.

'Sergeant Jones, Special Branch,' he snapped. 'What's happened?'

Inarticulately I gestured towards the open door in helpless despair. Without another word, Sergeant Jones sprang through and out onto the embankment.

Before I had a chance to recover myself, Mackenzie burst in followed by a person in female clothes – I dimly recognised some semblance of the shrill voiced woman who had accompanied Sergeant Jones – yet it was a man, a man holding a revolver.

Mackenzie took in the tableau at a glance.

'What's happened, Manders?' He demanded.

'She,' I gestured at Clarissa Walker's body, 'she was Fuchs. Lord Toby was one of the gang. Raffles and Lord Toby . . . fighting . . . fell off the train . . .'

Mackenzie swore.

'Is Jones out there?'

I affirmed that he was.

'Stay here, Roberts.'

The man in the woman's costume nodded.

Mackenzie had leapt onto the embankment ordering me to follow him.

I found myself plodding through cinders and stones along the side of the carriages. In the distance was a circling beam of light.

'Found them Jones?' barked Mackenzie.

'Not yet, sir,' came the north country voice.

We trotted down the track for several hundred yards, the cold night air soothing my shocked state so that I could briefly recount events to Mackenzie. He clucked his voice sympathetically.

'Sorry your wife's brother had to be mixed up in all this. I was frankly cynical when Raffles told me his suspicions. Clarissa Walker being *Frau* Fuchs comes as a complete surprise. Did Raffles recover the letters, by the way?'

I shook my head.

'I think Lord Toby had them on his person when he leapt out of the carriage.'

There was a cry ahead of us.

'Here, sir! Here they are!'

We broke into a trot and came to Sergeant Jones' side. He was kneeling by two black shapes.

Lord Toby Devenish lay in a small, twisted heap of clothing. His head seemed to be at an odd angle. Jones had a hand on his chest.

'This fellow is dead, chief,' he muttered.

Mackenzie grunted and began a search of Lord Toby's clothing.

Meanwhile Jones had shone his torch on the second black twisted shape. Raffles' face was pale and blood-stained. One arm was twisted behind him.

'He's still alive,' said Jones.

I gave a cry and bent down.

Jones had produced a small brandy flask and, with the aid of a handkerchief, was dabbing the liquid on Raffles' lips. His eyelids fluttered and he groaned.

'That . . . that you, Bunny?'

'It's me, old fellow,' I whispered hoarsely.

'Think I broke my arm. Did we get him?'

Just then Mackenzie gave a bray of triumph.

'The letters! Damn it, the letters!'

Raffles forced a grin.

'Devenish?'

'He's dead, Raffles,' I said. 'His neck was twisted by the fall.'

Raffles groaned and slumped unconscious.

'We'd best get him to a hospital, sir,' ventured Sergeant Jones.

Mackenzie pocketed the letters and nodded.

'I'll go back and get the train off. Roberts will take care of . . . Mrs Walker's body. You stay here, Manders. Sergeant Jones, we should be five or ten miles from Maidstone. See if you can find a telephone and get an ambulance from the local hospital.'

'Very good, sir.'

Mackenzie and Jones made off in opposite directions.

I tried to make Raffles as comfortable as I could, though I dared not try to straighten his twisted arm. Thoughtfully, Jones had left his brandy flask behind and we both needed it during the next hour or so of waiting.

It was nearly six o'clock. The sun was already climbing into the sky giving that strange ethereal light of early dawn, a coldness yet with a promise of warmth to come. I stared out on the hospital grounds from the whitewashed waiting room. It smelled overpoweringly of carbolic. It had taken Sergeant Jones a little time to summon an ambulance to bring Raffles to Maidstone Hospital. Mackenzie had caught the first train back to London to report to Sir Edward Carson on our success while I fretted and fumed in the waiting room for news of Raffles.

A thin faced man in a white coat finally looked in.

'Mister Manders?'

I swung round.

'How's Raffles?'

'He'll be all right. A broken arm, fortunately fractured cleanly so that it will mend easily enough; several minor contusions and a mild trace of concussion. Nothing that a good rest won't cure.'

I heaved a sigh of relief.

'You can go in and see him for a moment.'

I followed the doctor down a corridor into a small whitewashed room. Raffles lay in bed, his head wreathed in bandages and his left arm in a splint.

He forced a grin as I entered.

'What ho, Bunny.'

'How do you feel, Raffles?'

'Like death but I understand that I'll survive.'

'It seems so unreal,' I muttered.

He gave a slight nod.

'Sorry about Devenish. Sorry about Clarissa, I know you had a thing about her.'

I reddened.

'Not really,' I said coldly. 'It's Alice I'm worried about.'

In fact the subject had been spinning in my mind most of the time which had elapsed since Raffles' shocking revelation. Alice's brother was a spy – a traitor! My God! What would Alice say? What would I tell her?

'Poor Devenish,' muttered Raffles, closing his eyes. 'Want of money makes us all do strange things. Economics forces us into all manner of occupations we shouldn't ordinarily choose. Don't be too hard on the devil. He paid the piper.'

The doctor poked his head round the door,

' 'Fraid you'll have to go now. Mister Raffles needs some rest.'

I looked at the pale face against the pillow. It was

reposed, the eyes closed and the breath coming regularly. I turned and left the room silently.

Two days later I received a cablegram from Alice. She was returning home the next day, being delayed only by the necessity of winding up some business in Paris. A few laconic sentences informed me that our ambassador in Paris had called upon her and personally given her the news. But, apart from the brief statement of facts, there had been no mention of the part Raffles and I had played in tracking down her brother's part in the affair nor in the manner of his death. I was not sure how I could bring myself to tell Alice of that matter.

After I had breakfasted, I took a cab to Charing Cross and caught the train for Maidstone. I paused outside the grim grey portals of the hospital and purchased a box of chocolates. Then I made my way to Raffles' room.

I paused, startled on the threshold.

Seated beside Raffles, one hand in his, was the Baroness von Stalhein, her face was gazing at his with an expression akin to adoration.

Raffles turned his bandaged head towards me.

'Come in, Bunny, old chap.'

I took a pace forward.

'If you're busy, I can . . .' I began coldly.

'Not at all,' smiled Raffles. 'Inge was just leaving, weren't you darling?'

The Baroness smiled and stood up.

'Goodbye, liebling,' she positively cooed. 'I'll be back to see you tomorrow.'

With a nod in my direction, she left.

When she had gone I turned an indignant face to Raffles.

'Why isn't she under arrest?'

Raffles looked at me like a patient father trying to explain a simple problem to a backward son.

'After all the help she has given us?'

'Dash it all, Raffles!' I cried. 'The woman's a spy, an enemy of the country and all that.'

Raffles reached forward and took the box of chocolates from my hand, unwrapped it and sorted through for the hard centres which he was particularly fond of.

'There's a saying, old thing: better the spy you know than the spy you don't know.'

He grinned at my disgruntled expression.

'All right, Bunny,' he smiled. 'If you must know, Baroness von Stalhein has been persuaded to drop her allegiance to the Kaiser. She is, after all an Austrian. Following last weekend, I have induced her to throw in her lot with His Majesty's Secret Service.'

Confound the man! He actually had the audacity to wink at me when he said the word 'induce'.

'She is not to be prosecuted for her part in Fuchs' network?'

'No. Without her we would not have known that Fuchs and company were leaving the country on the Wednesday boat train. And she also told me about Lord Toby's part in the group, although she never knew about Clarissa Walker.'

My mouth dropped.

'So all the deduction you spouted about discovering Lord Toby was just a lot of nonsense?' I was aghast.

'More or less.'

Raffles lay back in bed and sighed.

'Fortunately, Inge, the Baroness that is, saw the error of her ways,' he reflected piously.

'Stuff and nonsense!' I muttered. 'The woman's fallen for you and I think you have gone quite soft on her.'

'And speaking of ladies,' Raffles changing the subject sharply, 'have you heard from Mrs Manders?'

I told Raffles about the cablegram from Alice.

'I hope she will understand when I tell her the details of this awful business,' I ended.

Raffles jerked up in bed with an abruptness that started me.

'Don't be an absolute ass, Bunny!' he snapped.

I was offended.

'You can't tell Alice about your part in the affair nor mine for that matter,' he explained patiently. 'You know nothing, except what the authorities tell you. You were not on the boat train that night. Understand?'

'No,' I retorted. 'Why can't I tell Alice? She has a right to know.'

'You have signed the Official Secrets Act. Not a word of your new employment nor the events of the last week can be told to a soul.'

I fell silent. Raffles was absolutely right, of course. I hadn't really thought about it. But, by the Lord Harry, it was going to be a difficult thing to live with. Poor Alice.

'Has Mackenzie discovered whether Devenish had any other motivation in spying for the Germans apart from money?' he asked, turning the conversation again.

Mackenzie and his men had been going through Lord Toby's papers both at his townhouse and Hurstdevenish.

'Money seems to be the main reason,' I replied. 'As you already discovered, the Devenish estates had been mortgaged several times in addition to which Lord Toby was an inveterate gambler. That seems to be why he sold himself to the German generals in the Wilhelmstrasse.'

'Money, eh?' mused Raffles. 'What a waste of talent. He was a deucedly clever chap, but too ruthless, too brutal. Money is the downfall of all those who don't have it.'

'And, of course, for the last two years he has been having an affair with Clarissa Walker.'

Raffles gave me a sympathetic glance.

'There was a cold blooded, ruthless woman, for you.'

'Well, I thank heavens that the beastly affair is over!' I said angrily, trying to hide my passions.

Raffles picked out another chocolate and grinned at me. I have seen that grin of anticipation many times before.

'I'm not sure that it is all over yet,' he said quietly.

I felt a coldness seize my stomach.

'What do you mean?' I demanded.

'Oh, it's just that I think that I've found a more exciting game than mere burglary. It's legal and just as financially rewarding.'

'You mean you *want* to be a spy?' I asked incredulously.

Raffles gave me a broad smile.

'I'm sure Sir Edward must have a number of little jobs in this line of business for someone of my talents. What about a new partnership, Bunny?'

187

'No!' I cried, leaping to my feet. 'By the Lord Harry, no!'

I stormed from the room. Of all the cheek! After what he had made me suffer! The very idea! Yet I had not progressed as far as the main doors of the hospital when a sinking feeling came over me. I knew the hold that Raffles was able to exert on me; knew he had only to set his mind to it and I would become his accomplice once again.

Raffles was right; Sir Edward would probably have a number of jobs lined up for us.